Giving You All I've Got

CENTRAL LIBRARY
0000208543645
AUSTIN PUBLIC LIBRARY

Love Me Forever

A Novel By:

A'zayler

Receiving: **[verb]** to take into one's possession; to be burdened with; sustain: to hold bear or contain: to take into the mind; apprehend mentally.

In life and even more in love, people tend to use the term "giving" more than they use "receiving," when in reality, they are equally important. For one to give successfully they must in return have someone on the receiving end. Love requires both. One must always be careful not to practice one more or less than the other. Though in most instances it seems easier to receive than to give, that's not always the case. Sometimes receiving something takes more courage than giving it, especially when its love.

I've had love. I've had love on many occasions. I've had so much love given that I'm no longer moved by its notion. The words, the actions, the excuses of love no longer matter to me. Why? Because it's doesn't mean anything. I've had so many people tell me that they love me, even show me for a little while that I've become quite used to it. However, just as I've had them give and show it, I've had them to disregard it and leave me as if that word means nothing.

So instead of holding on to the false hope that love makes you feel better, or does all of these unimaginable things that people speak on, I choose not to believe. I choose to keep my heart to myself and go through my everyday life just as I came into this world; with nothing. All of the things you say sounds good, but what good is it if I don't believe you? I mean, why should I? Why should I allow you to make me believe that your *I love you* is any different from the ones I've heard before? That's failure. I'm willingly setting myself up, and this time… this one time in my life… I'm choosing not to.

-Zino Green

Love to me, means everything. It's all I've ever wanted. I give it so freely sometimes that I end up having to take a step back to keep from giving it to the wrong people. In our relationship, I feel that's not the case. You are beautiful. You are amazing. You are damaged, but you are also mine. I'll never leave you. I don't want to… I couldn't. You've come along and made me want to heal the broken. Mend the tattered. Shelter the hurt from any more pain. I'll never allow anything else to bother your heart, because just like you, it is mine as well.

Forget the past, grab onto the future, and let me be your one. The one who erases the agony, nurtures the ruined, and replaces the fear of undeserving. You speak of unbelieving, but I think that's a lie. You're just afraid. You're afraid because of the past. You're afraid that if you open yourself to me that I'll be the same as the rest.

Well, my love, take my word when I say that I am not. I'm different.

I'm stronger. I'm fearless. I am love, and I am yours.

-Lonnie Bruce

Chapter 1: You should have known better

Was it his or Promise's? That one line resonated through Joc's head repeatedly as she lay across the bottom of Lu's bed. She had been in Georgia for almost a week and had spent majority of it at Lu and Brasi's spot. Though that hadn't been in her plans at all, she hadn't given herself much of a choice. Hell, neither had Uzoma.

After that one question found its way out into the atmosphere, things had been going downhill ever since, much like Joc had assumed it would. She'd always thought the news of her pregnancy rolling from Uzoma's sexy lips would make her feel better about the situation, but oh how wrong had she been. She felt even worse now than she had before.

Every day since finding out that she was indeed carrying her first child, Joc had been bummed out and unsure of how its arrival

1

would ruin her life. Now she knew. It would turn her into a crybaby, it would disturb every ounce of happiness she'd been working so hard to maintain, and most importantly, it would run off the one man who had shown the potential to love her the way she deserved to be loved.

Joc cringed again at the thought. Her stomach flip flopped and tightened in knots as the vision of his gorgeous face popped into her mind. Uzoma had been so different. He was the one who was going to show her that all men weren't the same. He was the one who had promised to be there for her no matter what, but now all of that was gone. Thanks to the little unwanted seahorse looking homewrecker that had made her womb its growing place for the next few months of its life.

Joc's hand ran over her abdomen again for the thousandth time that day. How had she allowed this to happen? It was all her fault. She'd known from the beginning that being with Uzoma was too good to be true.

"I don't know why in the hell you're laying your ass up in this room in the dark like it's going to make that damn baby disappear." Lu flipped the lights on before walking slowly over to the bed and sitting down. "You might as well get up and get your damn life. I'm sick of looking at you like this every day." Lu turned her nose up at Joc. "And bitch, go comb your damn hair."

Joc rolled over and tried to pull the covers over her head but was unable to because Lu was sitting on her blanket.

"For real, Joc, get up. This shit is ridiculous."

Joc huffed before throwing the covers off her body and sat up in the bed, slamming her back against the footboard roughly.

"Bitch, I don't care about you having no attitude. Just don't break my damn bed." Lu looked at Joc, not fazed at all by her little tantrum.

"You're getting on my fucking nerves." Joc sucked her teeth and rolled her eyes at Lu. "Crippled bitch."

The room was quiet for a minute before Lu and Joc both burst out laughing.

"Pregnant bitch," Lu countered once she'd caught her breath from laughing.

"Man, Lu, it's not funny." Joc sighed.

"I know it's not, but ain't nobody laughing about it, Joc."

Joc sat with her arms folded across her chest looking at her best friend. She was so miserable that she hadn't even given herself time to actually enjoy herself since she'd been there, and that wasn't like her at all. Whenever she and Lu were around each other, there were no limits to what they would get into. Sadly, this time had been totally different.

"What you think I should do?"

Lu twirled her walking cane around in front of her while looking down at the floor. "I don't know, but I can tell you what I think you shouldn't have done."

4

Joc shook her head and held her hand up in the air to stop her.

She didn't want to hear it. Lu had told her enough times since being

there what it was that she shouldn't have done, but it was too late

for that now. She had embarrassed herself enough, and did not plan

to continuing reliving it.

"Jocelynn, look…"

Joc slid back down into the bed and kicked around wildly like

a child. "Uzoma used to call me Jocelynn," she whined playfully.

"It sounded better when he said it."

Lu snickered a little before hitting Joc's legs. "Man, shut up Joc,

and get your behind out of this bed and go get the damn boy back

then."

"I don't think he wants me anymore."

"Well, you sure as hell aren't going to find out laying in here

like this."

Joc lay still, trying to think of what that she should do next. She and Uzoma hadn't spoken since the day she left his cousin's house in Columbus, and she'd been missing him terribly ever since. Just like it did every other time she thought about that night, his face and his words replayed in her head.

Was it his or Promise's?

The room was spinning for a second as Joc sat on the bed holding her head in her hands. Had he really just said what she thought he said? Her palms began to sweat as her stomach turned in crazy circles making her feel nauseous. Joc swallowed the rising saliva in her mouth, trying to find her voice, but she couldn't.

"Talk to me, Jocelynn." Uzoma's voice was hard but soothing to her nonetheless.

It was very clear that he was angry and was doing the best he could to contain it.

Joc looked up from the floor and made eye contact with him. "Talk to you?" she asked in disbelief.

Uzoma nodded. "Yes. Talk to me."

"What you want me to say, Uzoma?" She let her hands fall from the sides of her head and into her lap. "Huh? What you want me to say?"

He was still leaning against the back of the door with his long legs folded at the ankle. His face was unmoving and his posture was rigid as he stood as still as a statue waiting for her to answer his question. The sweat suit fitting his body in the most casual yet beautiful way. Joc's eyes roamed over his face that she could see much clearer thanks to the large ball he had all his hair pulled up into.

His bright skin adorned with freckles holding a reddish hue to it due to his obvious anger. The flawlessly shaped pink lips pouted out just enough to match the growing frown in his bushy brown eyebrows. How could someone be so perfect?

"I want you to answer my question. Is it mine or Promise's?"

There it was again. Joc's stomach flipped and did all the crazy stuff it had been doing since the topic arrived. Only this time along with it came a tinge of anger. The fuck did he mean was it his or Promise's? How in the fuck would it be Promise's? Was this nigga really standing there accusing her of being dumb enough to go back to Promise after she'd told him that she wouldn't?

Her legs began to shake again as her anger rose higher and higher. What kind of woman did he really think she was? Sure, she was a tad unstable mentally, and unsure of herself physicaly, but all of that was thanks to Promise's weak ass. Uzoma couldn't possibly think that she would actually go back there with Promise after the past two months of their relationship. Or could he?

"Joc, I don't plan to wait all night."

His tone of voice annoyed the shit out of her. She tried to calm herself down enough not to put her hands on him, because right then, in that moment, he was about to get his shit bust wide open accusing her of being dumb enough to double back with Promise.

"And I don't plan on making you wait all damn night, Uzoma."

Joc stood from the bed and snatched her purse and phone from the bed. "Take me back to the fucking airport or to the nearest bus station. I need to get away from your ass before I knock you the fuck out."

Joc leaned down to grab the handle of her suitcase and stood it up from the floor. Uzoma had her fucked up. She didn't have to take that shit. She was finna' go.

"Watch how you speak to me, Jocelynn."

"Why?" She looked at him like he was crazy. "You don't watch how you speak to me." She tried to mimic his African accent the best she could.

His left eye was jumping and he had crossed and uncrossed his ankles twice already, but none of that scared Joc. One thing she wasn't, was scared to fight a nigga. She and Promise had gone round for round on more than one occasion. She was more than positive she could hold her own with Uzoma as well.

9

"I won't tell you again," Uzoma told her before standing from the door and walking closer to her so that he was directly in front of her. "Now, I'm going to ask you again, and this will be the last time for that too."

Joc swallowed hard before looking off to the side. He was so intimidating. He made her sick. She was trying her hardest to stay mad, but he was so fine and always looked even better when he was angry. Especially when he got all demanding and shit.

"Is it mine or is it Promise's?" His hazel eyes bore into hers until she turned her head.

However, it didn't stay turned long. His hand on the back of her neck eased her face back around so that she was looking at him again. The tug on her neck was a bit forceful but not enough to hurt her or anything like that. Joc tried to fight eye contact as hard as she could but failed and ended up looking directly at him.

His face was solid and so was his touch. The steady breath releasing from his nose flowed out against her top lip and against

10

her cheek. The cologne he was wearing sifted up her nostrils as his chest grazed lightly against hers.

Being that close to him was making her feel like a punk bitch because versus going upside his head for accusing her of cheating, she wanted to kiss him, hug him, touch him, something other than give him a black eye. He licked his lips as he stared at her in that way that he always did, waiting for an answer.

"It's yours, Uzoma," Joc said quietly as his presence continued to diffuse her anger.

His chest sank as he released a breath that he had apparently been holding. His hand followed it and fell from her neck as he took a step back so that he could see her better. Joc stood still, waiting for him to say something else. He had been hounding an answer out of her for almost ten minutes, and he now he wanted to act speechless.

"Well?" Joc raised her eyebrow in question.

"How do I know that? You've been living up there with that

nigga the whole time we've been together. How do I know you didn't

mess around with him?"

Joc's chest sank this time. She was utterly flabbergasted by

Uzoma's reaction. She had not envisioned him acting like that. True

enough, she knew he would be shocked and may even have a few

questions, but treating her like a cheating liar was not it. For a

moment, she had even allowed herself to be happy about it upon

entering his cousin's house and seeing the love he had for his kids.

This was too much. Joc shook her head to the side trying to

shake back the tears as she gathered her things tighter in her hands

again and headed for the door. She tried her best to move past him

without making eye contact, but he wouldn't let her.

He had been standing in the middle of the floor but backed

up against the door again before she could get to it so that he could

block her path.

"Wait, Jocelynn." Both of his hands went to her arms.

"Get your hands off me, Uzoma."

"Where you going? Why you trying to run away from me?"
He sounded a little more somber that time.

Joc wanted to pity him and accept the comfort in his voice, but she was too angry. He had just disrespected her, and though he had a valid point about her living in Brooklyn, he still should have known better. At least known her well enough to know that she was happy with him and wouldn't dare run back to Promise and let the nigga knock her up.

"Can you take me to Lu's house?"

"To Lu's house? Why?" He grabbed her in a rush and looked at her like some sort of wounded puppy. "You really trying to leave me?"

"Yes." Joc sniffed the waiting snot back up into her nose. "I don't want to be here with you right now."

Uzoma's body tensed in front of her before he dropped both

13

of his hands from her arms. He took a few deep breaths before running his hand over his face.

"Let me tell my cousin, and then I'll take you."

Joc didn't say anything as he stepped around her to open the door. He stepped to the side to allow her room to go out first, handing her the car keys in the process. Joc took them with no problem and walked right past him. Even though she was no longer sure about going to Lu's house, she wouldn't let him see that. If he took her, then she would go.

She was walking down the hallway toward the front door they'd come in when his cousin's wife, Taryn, came back around the corner. She was smiling and no longer had the baby on her hip. That gave Joc the opportunity to see how thick the girl really was. Her hips and legs were big just like Joc's, and even though her belly was taking up most of her torso, Joc could still tell she was just as tall as she was too.

Taryn was so pretty. Pretty like a doll. Joc wished she was

14

effortlessly as pretty as Taryn was. That had to be easy.

"Where you going with your bags?" She gave Joc a concerned look before looking over her shoulder at Uzoma. Her face frowned deeper. "What the hell y'all went back there and did to each other? Y'all both looking crazy."

Joc shook her head softly from side to side, assuming Uzoma would answer for them both, but he was just as quiet as she was. Her eyes rolled as she thought about how she should have known. He was the same one who wasn't sure about bringing her to see his family, he most definitely wasn't going to scream to the world that she was pregnant by him. Hell, let him tell it, pregnant by Promise.

"Uzoma, what did you do to this girl?" Taryn put her hands on her hips, stopping them both from exiting the hallway.

"How you know it was me that did something?"

Taryn shrugged then looked at Joc. "Was it you?"

Joc looked down at the floor before shaking her head again.

15

"Girl, I don't even know."

The hallway was a little quiet as the three of them stood there waiting for someone to provide some sort of clarity. When nothing came, Taryn shook her head and turned around.

"Demoto!" she yelled. "Uzoma and his girlfriend are leaving. I don't know what the hell happened that fast, but they're leaving," she continued to yell as she walked back in the direction she had just come from.

Even being as bothered as she was right then, Joc couldn't do anything but laugh. She snickered lightly as she watched Taryn wobble back toward the front of their home. This too gave her another opportunity to admire Taryn. Her butt was huge like Joc's, and her hair was long and wavy in a pattern similar to Joc's. If she didn't know any better, she would have thought Uzoma had gotten himself a knockoff Taryn.

"You can head to the car. I'll let them know what's up." Uzoma maneuvered past her.

16

"Let them know as in blaming me for being pregnant by another nigga, or you accusing me of being a liar and cheater?" Joc knew that was petty, but she couldn't stop herself.

Uzoma looked at her with disdain. "Just go to the car."

"You don't tell me what to do."

He looked at her for a few moments longer before releasing a frustrated breath and continuing in the direction that Taryn had just gone in. Joc pulled her bag behind her, headed for the door She could hear talking going on in what she assumed to be the kitchen before opening the door.

The moment the door was open, a loud alarm went off, scaring the life out of her. Joc grabbed her chest and jumped in fear as the loud noise rang out through the house. She hurried to close the door, thinking that was going to help, but it didn't. The alarm was still sounding throughout the house.

It took a few seconds, but it eventually stopped. She was still in

17

the same spot when Demoto came around the corner. His stride was

the exact replica of Uzoma's. He was so tall and moved with so

much ease, if she hadn't been looking at him, she would have never

known he was coming.

His long hair fell over his shoulders as he moved toward her.

His face was hard and unreadable, which only made her even more

nervous than she had already been after the alarm sounded. Once

he got to her, he stepped past her and locked the door back.

"Don't leave. Let's eat." He was short and to the point, just like

Uzoma.

"I'm okay."

Demoto raised an eyebrow at her. "Girl, stop acting up and

bring your ass in this kitchen and eat. My wife been cooking for y'all

all day. Ain't no way y'all about to dip without at least eating some

of that shit."

He only gave her his attention for a few more seconds before turning to walk away. Joc stood there stuck, unsure of what to do. On a normal basis, she didn't take orders from anybody, but clearly that was some African shit because that was the same way that Uzoma walked around talking to people.

She didn't understand why he did it any more than she understood why Demoto thought she was about to listen to him. Who did he think he was? Better yet, who did he think she was? Joc rolled her eyes and looked up at the ceiling to take a few deep breaths.

When she looked back down, she looked directly into Taryn's face. She was peeking around the corner. Upon realizing she'd just been caught by Joc, she smirked and quickly jumped back around the corner. A light snicker eased from Joc as she set her things against the wall and headed for the kitchen.

She was really hating that their first impression of her would be a crazy one, but she honestly had no real control over that right then. Uzoma was the fool that wanted to act out and embarrass them in front of his family. All of their talking ceased the moment she

19

walked into the kitchen.

Taryn was standing at the counter making plates of food while Demoto, Uzoma, a dread headed little boy, and the baby girl she'd seen earlier sat at the table. The baby girl was nestled against Demoto's chest while he fed her the food that was in the little pink bowl in front of her.

Uzoma sat opposite of Demoto and his children on the other side of the table. Next to him was an empty chair that she assumed was left for her. Uzoma and Demoto both looked up at her when she remained standing at the door.

"You not sitting down?" Demoto asked her.

"I was about to," Joc sassed, drawing a snicker from Taryn.

"She said she's about to, Demoto, with your nosey ass." Taryn walked over to Joc and grabbed her arm. "Don't let that nigga try to intimidate you. Ain't nobody scared of his ass."

"It's alright, Uzoma does me the same way."

"Girl, it's that African blood. They're bossy as shit. My son is the same way, and he's a kid. I be having to remind that lil nigga who's in charge sometimes." Taryn laughed. "Demoto got him thinking he's my second daddy."

"Nah, my son just knows to look out for you when Daddy ain't around." Demoto stuck his fist out and the little boy gave him a pound. "Ain't that right, Ayo?"

"Yes sir." The little boy nodded his head while chomping on his chicken leg.

Taryn ushered Joc to her chair and pulled it out for her before walking away to grab the plates she'd fixed from the counter. While she was away, Joc looked around the table at the babies. They were the cutest kids she'd ever seen. So beautiful, like their parents.

Taryn moved around until she'd given everybody their food before sitting down. She looked over at Joc and smiled before nodding her head toward Uzoma. That nigga hadn't said a word to her since she'd been in the kitchen. Joc turned her nose up and

21

rolled her eyes, making Taryn laugh.

"Man, y'all need to stop y'all mess and just enjoy being here. Whatever it is, I'm sure it's not that bad," Taryn said.

"That's him," Joc referred to Uzoma who was busy eating the rice and corn on his plate.

"You're the one talking about leaving me, so..." He looked at her once. His expression just as solemn as his voice had been. "What you want me to say?"

Taryn stopped eating and looked at them both with a sympathetic expression. "Aww, Joc, why you say that?"

"Because he doesn't want me."

Uzoma tossed his fork down and looked at her. "What? Now why would you say some shit like that?"

Joc looked down but didn't say anything. She didn't really mind letting his family know that she was pregnant, but she wasn't sure if he did, and she was in no mood to make things between them

22

any worse than they already were.

"See, that's how you know it was her. She can't even say nothing," Demoto said aloud.

"Shut up, Moto," Taryn told him before Joc could say anything in her defense.

"Jocelynn." Uzoma grabbed her leg beneath the table.

When she sat looking at her plate, he squeezed her thigh a little tighter. "Look at me," he whispered.

It took her a minute, but when she finally did, he was staring her down with eyes like rivers of love. They were so potent and mesmerizing. Like hazel streams of emotion.

"You think I don't want you?" His voice was very quiet, but Joc was more than positive his family could still hear him.

Joc shrugged.

He cleared his throat and moved his hand from her thigh to her back and rubbed it up and down. He ran his hand through her ponytail before leaning over and kissing the side of her face.

"I want you."

The subtle sigh from Taryn confirmed Joc's thoughts of them being able to hear him. It was crazy to Joc how it didn't seem like he cared in the least that they could hear him talking to her. Most men would never say those types of things out loud, but clearly Uzoma wasn't most men.

"I want you so fucking much." He kissed her ear before biting it lightly. "You hear me?"

Joc nodded as she fought back a smile.

"You still want me?"

Again, Joc nodded.

"Well, tell me then." His arm was still around her when he pulled her over to him.

Her body leaned slightly out of her chair as she whispered against his neck. "I want you, Uzoma." Unlike him, expressing her feelings wasn't something she knew how to do without shame, so she really did whisper it.

Uzoma pulled away and looked at her after she kissed his neck. When they made eye contact again, he kissed her mouth before letting her go so that she could sit back upright in her chair.

"I love y'all. Oh my God!" Taryn shrieked when Joc was back upright in her chair. "Y'all are so cute."

"Girl, shut your dramatic ass up, making all that damn noise." Demoto tossed a noddle of macaroni at her.

"Leave me alone, Moto. They're cute." Taryn rested her chin in the palm of her hand and continued watching them.

She was so silly. She kept Joc laughing throughout dinner and well into the evening. They ended up laughing and talking so much that she and Uzoma had put their things back into the guest room

25

and decided to stay. They were well into the night and chilling in their pajamas when the doorbell rang.

Joc and Uzoma were cuddled up in the large recliner while Demoto and Taryn had taken the love seat. Demoto paused their movie and got up to answer the door. When he came back there was a smaller framed brown skinned girl following him in a pair of spandex pants and a tight exercise top. She was pretty, with a short haircut.

"Every time I come over here your fat ass laid up like a fucking cow," she told Taryn with her face frowned.

"Fuck you, hoe. What you want this late anyway?" Taryn replied. "And what the hell you got on? It's cold outside"

"Mind your business, bitch. I just left the gym." The girl walked over to the computer desk in the corner. "I told Jack I would stop and get his schedule from Moto so he didn't have to bring my baby back out of the house."

26

"Joc, this is my rude ass best friend Kia. Kia, this is Uzoma's girlfriend, Joc."

Joc giggled because she'd thought she and Lu were the only two people in the world who talked to each other that way.

"Oh, hey girl. I forgot Taryn told me y'all were coming." She waved and smiled at Joc.

"Hey. It's nice to meet you."

Kia's face frowned briefly. "Girl, where you from?"

"Brooklyn."

Kia nodded. "I should have known. I like your accent."

"How should you have known? You been there before?" Uzoma asked Kia, totally rubbing Joc the wrong way.

It wasn't even about what he said, but the way he'd said it. Something about it sounded too flirtatious for Joc's liking. Not to mention, Kia wasn't even talking to his ass. He'd gone out of his way to speak to her. Not that Joc wanted him to be rude to the girl,

but damn, speaking when spoken to worked just fine for Joc.

Kia giggled. "Uzoma, don't start with me tonight. You know I

don't play with your ass."

He chuckled deeply. "Yeah. We'll see about that."

The fuck?

Joc shifted some in her seat as she felt the back of her neck

getting hot. That nigga was really trying her.

"We'll see then, nigga." Kia giggled again before she headed

back toward the door. "Fertile Myrtle come lock the door behind

me," she yelled over her shoulder to Taryn.

When Taryn tried to get up, Demoto stopped her, letting her

know that he would do it. Joc had been watching the way he was

always so careful and loving with Taryn the entire night. It was

definitely a sight to see, and she wanted to see more of it, but Uzoma

had her fucked up.

He wasn't going to sit there and play her like she was some kind of fool. She wasn't blind, she could tell flirting when she saw it. Then he had the nerve to do it so blatantly. All that meant was that he and Kia had probably messed around in the past. It was obvious.

Joc was so worked up that when he put his arm back around her, she pushed it right back off her. She could feel him looking at her out of the corner of her eye, but she wasn't paying him any attention. Nor had she paid him any attention that night or the next day either. She spoke to him long enough to tell him she was ready to go to Lu's house and that was it.

Uzoma was pissed as hell, which was probably why he brought up the baby situation once again. Joc tried her best not to let his words hurt her feelings, but she couldn't help it. They did, and had been since then.

"So, what you gon' do? You going to get your man or what?" Lu asked her again.

Joc thought about it for a minute before nodding her head and hopping from the bed. "Hell yeah, I'm going to get his ass."

Chapter 2: I should have handled it better

"I think you should go see her," Taryn said as she wrapped the scarf around her neck.

Uzoma and Demoto had been sitting in the living room playing the game when she walked in. She was dressed and preparing to go to her doctor's appointment.

"I think you should get out of this man's business," Demoto told her.

"Hush, Moto." She pulled her hat down over her head. "So, you going to get her or what, Uzoma?"

Uzoma looked at Taryn before shrugging. "She the one wanted to wild on me about stupid shit."

"Well, since you still ain't told nobody what y'all were arguing

31

about, I can't really form an opinion on whether or not her reasoning was stupid. You know how y'all men are. You probably did something to that girl."

Uzoma was still playing the game as he listened to Taryn plead Joc's case for her. He'd thought about telling Taryn about the baby and the Kia situation the night he returned to Columbus from dropping her off at Lu's house but chose not to.

He didn't want to put something like that out into the atmosphere only to have to take it back in the end if he found out that Joc's baby wasn't his for real. He'd heard her tell him that it was, but he wasn't sure. In the back of his mind he knew it was his, but the nagging doubt in his chest wanted to believe that she had cheated with Promise.

Uzoma was too afraid to take her word for it and allow it to pain him in the end. At first, he'd thought he was strong enough to have that conversation with her, but once he saw how angry she'd gotten, he was weakened. The anger that she displayed should have convinced him that she was telling the truth, but he'd been down that road before, taking a woman's word, and he had been wrong.

"Why she mad?" Taryn took a seat on the arm of the chair.

"You might as well tell her. She ain't gon' let it go." Demoto paused the game.

Uzoma tossed his controller to the side and lay back against the sofa cushion. He inhaled a deep breath before looking over at Taryn.

"She's pregnant."

"For real?" Taryn shrieked with excitement.

Uzoma nodded.

"It's yours?" Demoto asked with his eyebrow raised.

"That's the same thing I asked her, and she went off."

Demoto and Uzoma both started laughing, but stopped when Taryn stood up and slapped both of them upside their head.

"Don't do that shit. It's not funny. Demoto, I wish you would

33

have asked me some mess like that, and Uzoma, you need to be ashamed of yourself."

He frowned. "Why I got to be ashamed because I want to know?"

"Do you really think she would have cheated, got pregnant by somebody else, and then told you about it?"

"She didn't tell me. I asked her about it."

"Why she ain't tell you?" Taryn pulled her hat off her head and sat back down.

"You might as well put that hat right back on your damn head. We got to go check on my baby. We ain't got time to be this nigga's counselor." Demoto got up and took her hat from her hand before placing it back on her head.

Uzoma watched them. Their love was so inspiring. It was one of the main reasons why he had been on his head to find him a good girl to settle down with. Taryn and Demoto had been through some serious shit, and to see the way they rocked through it had made him want the same thing, or at least something similar.

Taryn swatted at Demoto's hands, pushing him out of her face. "Why she ain't tell you, Uzoma?"

"She didn't know I knew."

Demoto and Taryn both looked at him with questioning expressions.

"How she not know you knew?" Taryn asked. "That's weird."

Uzoma stretched his legs out in front of him. He wasn't too sure what Taryn was going to think about what he was about to tell her, but then again, she was married to Demoto. Not much should still surprise her.

"I had her followed."

Taryn's frown deepened. "You got somebody spying on that girl?"

"Not necessarily. I don't have them spying on her, just looking out for her. I like to know she's safe when I'm not there."

Taryn shook her head from side to side. "You and Demoto really are brothers. I swear y'all have no limits when it comes to other people's privacy."

"Privacy? You don't need no privacy from me, Tee," Demoto told her.

Uzoma chuckled. If only she knew Demoto had been the one to hook him up with the person that he had trailing Joc, she would really have something to say then.

"I would think that was sweet if I didn't think it was crazy." She stood to her feet.

Uzoma shrugged. "Once she left the doctor, I had her records pulled and found out."

"How you do that? That's against the law." Taryn was looking at him, but stopped as realization crossed over her face. "Demoto

36

Youngblood, why do I feel like you had something to do with invading this girl's privacy?"

"I just told you, Tee, I don't believe in privacy, and if my brother is about to get serious about this girl for real, then I don't believe in it for her ass either." He shrugged as if it was no big deal.

Taryn sucked her teeth. "Y'all make me sick... Uzoma, go get that damn girl. That's your fucking baby and you know it."

"How he know?"

"How I know?"

He and Demoto asked at the same time.

"Because if any other nigga had been over there to have sex with her and leave his baby, y'all spying asses would already have known that." She shook her head as she grabbed her things so she could leave the house. "Y'all dumb asses. Y'all think y'all so smart that you're stupid."

"Aye, girl, don't make me beat your ass." Demoto slapped her

37

butt.

"Nigga, please." She looked from him to Uzoma. "But Uzoma, I thought y'all had got over that at the dinner table? How y'all start back arguing?"

He released a frustrated sigh. "She said I was flirting with Kia."

"What?" Demoto said in disbelief.

Uzoma nodded, acknowledging his agreement with Demoto's reaction.

"Well, I don't know about all of that, but I will say you was doing a bit much. I had thought it, but I wasn't going to say nothing." Taryn looked off to the side. "Had that been Demoto flirting with one of Joc's friends, I would have knocked his ass out right then."

"I ain't even say nothing!" Uzoma sounded exasperated.

"It ain't what you said, it's how you said it, but hey…" She shrugged. "What do I know?"

After that, she grabbed her phone and left the house with Demoto in tow. He and Uzoma shared an amused look before he told him that they would be back later. Uzoma sat in the silence of their home trying to think about whether he was about to go get Joc.

He hadn't thought about it before, but Taryn was right. He had been having her tailed since the first weekend he'd ever been to Brooklyn. After running into Promise and seeing what kind of nigga he was, Uzoma hadn't felt secure enough to leave her up there alone, so he'd had Demoto send a friend he'd worked with in the past from Double O to look after her.

The day he'd found out that she was pregnant, he had been ecstatic. Though he had wanted them to be in a better predicament before bringing a child into their lives, he was still happy. A baby with her was perfect. When he had allowed the doubt that it could have been Promise's to come into his mind, he couldn't remember, but he hated that he had.

Uzoma had been feeling bad about it since the day he'd taken

39

her and dropped her off. He wasn't sure what he should do anymore. It had always been in his nature to fight for what he wanted, but for some reason, Joc was making him second guess himself.

Should he fight for her, or just give her some space? He didn't want to crowd her, but he didn't want to run her off either. His mind was in turmoil as he allowed his thoughts to get the best of him. Before he knew it, twenty minutes had passed and he was still sitting in the same spot.

By the time he got up and decided that he was driving to Lu's house to get his girl, it had been a full thirty minutes since Taryn and Demoto had left. He looked around their house as he headed to the room he'd been sleeping in to get his things. If he ever wanted a love like theirs, then he had to give Jocelynn all he had.

***

Uzoma sat on the sofa waiting for Joc and Lu to come back from the mall. He had arrived at Brasi's house a while ago but had been waiting for her ever since. After Brasi told him that they had gone to the mall to get their hair and nails done, he made himself comfortable and prepared to wait.

"Lu just hit me, letting me know they were outside and to come get her bags and shit," Brasi told him as he stood from the chair he had just been sitting on.

Uzoma nodded and stood to follow him outside. Though he couldn't see Joc through the dark tint of Lu's jeep, he knew she was looking at him; he could feel it. Not only did they have that strong of a connection, but he knew had it been him he would have been staring her down.

Once he was on the side of the jeep he assumed she was on, he opened the door and helped her out. She looked a little skeptical as she gave him her hand, but got herself together once she was standing upright on her feet in front of him.

"You had fun shopping?" he asked as he examined the freshly arched brows on her face. "I like your hair." He ran his hand through the silky straight mane adorning Joc's head.

41

"Thank you," she said, just above a whisper.

Uzoma's hand still on her head massaging her scalp might have been what was taking her nerve, so he continued. He needed to disarm her if he wanted to make things right between them. Let Taryn tell it, he had been the one in the wrong, so he needed to do everything he could to make her feel better.

He hadn't thought anything of the remarks he made to Kia, but after giving it a little more thought, that hadn't been the smartest thing to do with Joc still having self-esteem issues. That had actually been one of the worst. Here he was supposed to be the one helping her get over that shit, and he was adding to it.

Uzoma leaned his head forward and held up some of her hair to smell it. "You been thinking about me?"

"Hey to you too, Uzoma," Lu said from behind them.

He looked up at her with Joc's hair still in his hand. He smiled at Lu. "My fault, Lu. How you doing?"

"Don't try to speak now, nigga, with your smiling ass." She smiled at him. "My bestie got you cheesing like that?"

Uzoma looked down at Lu hard and seductively. "That and some," he told Lu.

"I told you my best friend was the shit." Lu giggled as Brasi ushered her into the house.

Uzoma hadn't torn his gaze from Joc yet, and had no plans to do so. She was so gorgeous, and it was truly a waste that she didn't know it.

"I asked you have you been thinking about me." He let her hair go and grabbed the side of her neck.

"Every day."

Uzoma grabbed both sides of Joc's neck and leaned his forehead against hers. "I've been thinking about you every day, every night, every second. I miss you."

"Well, why haven't you called? Text? Anything?"

"I was being a fool. Do you forgive me?"

Joc nodded and stood on her tip toes so that she could kiss him. Uzoma grabbed her whole body into his arms and pulled her against his chest. His tongue slipped deep into her mouth, taking back the feeling that he'd been missing since she'd left. Her body relaxed against his as he held onto hers.

Joc's fingers ran through his hair, tugging and massaging here and there. He pushed her backward so that she was leaning against the jeep as he rubbed up and down her butt and thighs. Joc was breathing heavily as she desperately held onto him Uzoma. The eagerness that she felt for him was all through her kiss.

Though he was enjoying Joc's kiss, he needed to see her face. Uzoma pulled away just enough so that he could look at her.

"Don't leave me again." He pecked her lips. "Okay?"

Joc nodded before pulling him back to her and assaulting his lips some more. She felt so good in his arms, Uzoma couldn't see how he'd let her go in the first place.

"Hold on, wait." Joc pulled away and pushed him backward some. "What about the baby Uzoma?"

He could tell she wasn't really sure about talking about their child to him, which made him feel like an even bigger asshole, but she had to know. The way she rushed it out in such a hurry let him know that she had to say it before she lost her nerve.

"Our baby?" He kissed her forehead. "What about our baby?"

Joc's eyes misted when she smiled at him. He pulled her to him and hugged her head to his chest. "Don't worry about our baby, it'll be straight. What you need to worry about is if you're ready to leave your daddy in Brooklyn because you're coming down here with me." He kissed the top of her head a few times before making eye contact with her. "Y'all have to come live here with me. I'm not letting you or my kid stay away from me like that."

"Uzommmmaaa," she dragged.

"Uzoma nothing. I let you do that shit long enough, but now that you got my baby, you can kiss that shit goodbye."

"I'm not ready to move yet."

"You'll get ready." His gaze was intent.

She needed to know he was serious. He had allowed her to stay in Brooklyn for the first few months of their relationship due to the fact that they were still building and getting to know one another, but now all of that was going out of the window. He wouldn't dare have her and his baby states away from him. He'd never get any sleep like that.

"You're so demanding."

He pecked her nose. "You'll get used to it eventually."

"I hope so." She looked up at him with stars in her eyes as he looked back down at her. "You sure about this?"

His eyebrows frowned momentarily. "Sure about what?"

"The baby?"

"There's nothing to be sure about. You're my girl, and you're having my baby. I should have handled it better from the beginning."

"It's okay." Joc looked down and shuffled her feet.

"No, it's not. You were right not to let me disrespect you." He pulled away and looked around outside for a moment. "You have any more plans for today?"

"Well I was on my way to come get you, but since you beat me to it, I guess not."

Uzoma's face blushed red when he heard her tell him that she was on her way to get him. He liked that. She had just as much fight in her as he had in him. He was so outdone, he couldn't even stop himself from blushing. When he looked at her, she was smiling bashfully.

"You make me crazy, beautiful girl." His arms were back around her, pulling her to him.

47

"You make me happy, beautiful boy."

Uzoma chuckled at her response before grabbing her things from the jeep and putting them into his rental truck. When he was finished, they gathered the rest of her things from the house before letting Lu and Brasi know that they were about to go. Once they were back in the truck and buckled in, Uzoma pulled out, headed back to Columbus.

"So, where are you making me move to? Here with Lu and Brasi them or Columbus with your family?"

"Columbus," he told her without hesitation.

"Why there?" She turned her nose up.

"Because its small and safe for us. I'm pretty much done doing foot work here with Brasi, so I can relocate."

"I don't know anything about Columbus." Joc pouted.

Uzoma grabbed her hand and held it in his. "Well, neither do I, so I guess that means we'll have to figure it all out together."

Joc looked out of the window and nodded her head. Uzoma's eyes trailed down from her face, to her neck, and then to her breasts. They looked so appetizing in her sweater. His gaze lowered a little more, landing on her thighs. He tried his best to look quickly before returning his eyes back to the road.

It had been almost a week since she'd left him in Columbus, and a few weeks before then since he'd last seen her, and he needed some pussy bad. The way she looked and smelled was making it hard for him to think about the ride back to Columbus without getting any ass before then.

Uzoma wasn't sure how she was going to feel about his next move, but he didn't give a fuck. The moment he saw the exit that had Walmart on it, he got off. He drove until they were in the packed Walmart parking lot and parked toward the back. He killed the engine before locking the doors and looking over at her.

"Why we here?" she asked him.

"Come give me a kiss."

Joc sat in her seat for a minute before giving him a sly smile.

"Your nasty ass." She giggled. "You don't want no kiss, you want some butt."

"Well, give me some then."

Joc smiled as she looked around the parking lot. "We're too big for this, Uzoma."

"I'ma let the seat back, you just get on top and make it worth it."

Joc sat in her seat smiling for only a few more seconds longer before Uzoma reached out and grabbed her hand.

"Come on, Jocelynn. I need you, baby." His voice sounded pained, almost agonizing as he stared at her, waiting for her to welcome him into her body again.

Joc's mouth parted some as he watched her facial expression change. She looked so hot that he could hardly contain himself. He wanted to be buried so deep inside of her that he could touch her heart with the tip of his dick.

"You're so fucking overpowering, Uzoma. Damn." Joc fanned herself before unbuttoning her jeans.

His eyes caught sight of her thick brown thighs as she pulled them from her legs and let them fall to the floor. The way they spread across his seat made him bite his bottom lip. He watched her intently before reaching over and grabbing the side of her panties and pulling at them hungrily.

He wasn't exactly sure what he was trying to do right then, tear them off, or help her get them down. All he knew was that he wanted them off.

"Hurry up, Jocelynn. Let me see it, baby."

She licked her lips coyly. "See what, Uzoma?"

"Your pussy, baby girl. Get on top and let me look at you."

Her chest sank and she rolled her eyes to the back of her head as she pulled her panties down. Once they were off, he snatched them from her and held them in one of his hands as he helped her climb over the armrest with the other one.

It took them a good minute to get in a comfortable position, and it was starting to annoy Uzoma. Her body was too close to him for him not to be in it already. It was like every time the tip of his dick grazed her opening or touched the inside of her thigh as she tried to situate herself, he nearly exploded.

Uzoma slapped Joc's ass out of frustration. "Come on, Jocelynn, let me get up in there, baby." He closed his eyes as he pleaded. "Please…"

"You don't have to beg, baby." She moaned as she finally slid down on top of him.

Uzoma's entire body shuddered as he tried to keep himself from busting too early. Her tight, wet walls welcomed him immediately. They were pulling and squeezing him as if her body had missed him just as much as he'd missed her.

"Awww, fuck." Uzoma shivered again when he felt her mouth on his neck.

"Yeah, you missed me," she boasted and licked his neck again.

Uzoma wanted to say something slick and freaky to her, but the way she had him feeling right then, he couldn't think of shit to say. All he wanted to do was lay back and enjoy the feel of her surrounding him. Since there wasn't much moving room, she was barely moving, but not even that mattered.

In her current position, her breasts were directly in his face. Uzoma grabbed two handfuls and groped them shamelessly. He wanted to feel her any way that he could. When touching was no longer enough, he lifted her shirt and bra and covered her breasts with his mouth.

"Ahhhh…" She arched her back as the warm moisture from his mouth circled her nipples. "Uzomaaa," she moaned into his ear.

Yeah, this was that shit. Jocelynn had the kind of love he had to be in day in and day out. There would definitely be no more Brooklyn for her. She could go get all her stuff, but that was it. She was moving her ass back to Georgia. With pussy like that, he was surprised that he hadn't gotten her pregnant faster. Every time he was inside he felt like he was handicapped.

"Somebody gon' see us, baby," Joc whispered to him again as she looked down into his face.

"Let 'em see. As beautiful as you are, the world needs to fucking see."

She leaned forward, trying to hug him, but only pressed her breasts further into his face. Never the one to complain, Uzoma grabbed onto her ass and went back to licking and sucking on her nipples. He and she were both so enthralled in their lovemaking that he had completely forgotten they were in the parking lot of Walmart until he heard a tap on his window.

Joc's entire body stilled as she buried her face into his neck.

Uzoma looked over toward where the knock had come from and there was a man standing there giving him the thumbs up. Why in the fuck had he done that? What had been his point for doing that shit?

It angered Uzoma to no end that he'd interrupted him, and because he was more than certain he had gotten a good glimpse of Joc's ass. Though he'd told her that he wanted the world to see, he hadn't meant that shit literally. There was no way in hell he would ever put her out like that to be ogled by the filthy men of the streets.

The more he thought about it, the angrier he got. Before he knew it, he was no longer in the mood to have sex. He pushed Joc back a little because he could feel his dick deflating, and she needed to get dressed.

"Slide off and get dressed. That nigga just ruined my fucking mood."

Joc looked at Uzoma. "For real?"

"Yeah, for real. Standing his ass there with his thumb up like I need his fucking approval or some shit," Uzoma fumed. "Lame niggas like that make me sick."

Joc laughed as she removed herself from his lap and got back into her seat. Uzoma handed her the black lace panties he had been holding in his hand and fixed himself as he watched her get dressed. She snickered and made sly little comments the whole time she got dressed, while he sat in his seat fuming.

"Uzoma, it ain't that serious, baby. We don't even know that damn man."

"That's what I'm saying. We don't know his ass, yet he felt compelled to knock on my fucking glass and interrupt my nut." Uzoma cranked the truck back up, clearly flustered. "That just blew the fuck out of me."

Joc giggled even harder at him as he drove them toward the highway. Her laughter eventually calmed him down enough for him to indulge in laughter as well.

56

"Man, you wild."

"And you're crazy as hell. How are you going to get mad about somebody seeing us in a Walmart parking lot? You had to know somebody was going to see my big ass through that window."

Uzoma had been laughing, but stopped the moment she referred to herself in a negative way. "Why you had to add that?"

"Because it's the truth, Uzoma, chill." She smiled and tried to wave him off, but that had made him mad as hell.

"Nah, it ain't alright, and it ain't the truth. I mean, yeah, you do have a big ass, but not in the sense that you were saying it." He cut his eyes at her as he drove. "Don't do that no more, Jocelynn, and I'm not playing with you."

"Don't do what?"

"Don't speak about yourself in a negative way. You hear me?" He raised his voice a little.

Joc nodded and turned to look out the window. She was quiet

for a long time. She was so quiet that he almost felt bad for going so hard on her. Even though it was for a good reason, he still wasn't trying to hurt her feelings.

"I didn't mean to yell, I just don't like for you to talk about yourself like that. You're way more than you know, Jocelynn. If you'd acknowledge that for yourself, there wouldn't be shit nobody else could say to you." He grabbed her hand. "You've got to see that, baby."

She nodded. "I know. I'm fine."

"How fine are you?"

"Fine-fine," she joked.

"Good." He pulled her hand to his mouth to kiss.

For the rest of their ride back to Columbus they laughed and talked about a little bit of everything. By the time they got there, Taryn and Demoto were back home, and Uzoma could tell by the look on Taryn's face that she approved of his actions.

Chapter 3: Will you be my Valentine?

"You looking for something for your girlfriend?" the light skinned female with the jet black hair standing next to Zino asked.

She had been trying her hardest to be discreet as she stood and watched him stare at the boxes of colorful chocolate candy. He'd noticed her as soon as she joined him on the aisle. Even with her damn near going blind trying to look at him out of the corner of her eye, he'd spotted her.

He had been so accustomed to watching people in his past life, there was no way some random woman who thought he was cute would be able to get past him. On top of that, they were the only two people on the aisle. He had only been in Walmart for a few minutes looking for a box of Apple Jacks cereal when the candy aisle caught his attention.

Valentine's Day was quickly approaching, and he hadn't given it two thoughts until passing that aisle. After all, it wasn't like he had a real Valentine. Well, not in his opinion. He and Lonnie had been kicking it pretty tough for the past few weeks, but he still hadn't labeled it anything more than a friendship.

"If you are, I think you should get her Snickers. That's my favorite. It's probably hers too." The girl tried her luck at getting his attention again.

Zino finally gave her what she was looking for and looked over at her. She was smiling bashfully, clearly satisfied with his appearance. His eyes trekked up and down her body, observing her mediocre frame before landing back on her face.

"I don't have a girlfriend. I just like candy," hHe stated bluntly.

She smiled even harder before nodding her head and looking off to the side. "Well, maybe you should get you one. It would be such a misfortune to be single on Valentine's Day."

60

"Where your man at, shawty?" Zino decided to cut to the chase.

He was in no real mood for small talk. There was nothing she could say that would get him to make her his girlfriend. He wasn't with that shit, and that was it. He didn't mind hitting her off with some dick and a hug or two, but that was all he was offering.

"I don't have one."

"Well, who you getting candy for?"

She shrugged. "I might just like candy too."

Zino almost turned his nose up at her because it was obvious as fuck that she had a nigga that she was trying to hide for his benefit, which she didn't have to do. He would have fucked her even if she had told him she had a nigga. That ain't have shit to do with him.

"Cool. What you about to do?"

"I don't know. How about I give you my number and you hit me up later when you're free?"

"Cool." Zino handed her his phone and watched her enter her name and number before handing it back to him.

She was still smiling when he grabbed a bag of heart shaped snickers and left the aisle. He wasn't quite sure what Lonnie's favorite candy was, but maybe it was Snickers. Whether it was or it wasn't, he was going to give them to her. Either she liked them or she didn't.

The two lines that were actually open in Walmart were long as hell, so he took his cereal and Lonnie's candy and headed toward the self-checkout. After he rang his things up, he left. He checked his watch as he headed to the car. Lonnie would be getting off in another twenty minutes, so he had a few minutes to burn.

He'd planned on asking her to go out to eat with him. Not a date, just two hungry people sharing a meal and a table. That was the easiest way to look at it, in his opinion. Zino had been trying his hardest not to get too attached to her because though she was sweet and easy to get along with, he wasn't with that girlfriend shit.

Especially with Lonnie.

She was so big on family that it irritated him sometimes. Not to the point where he would give her a hard time about spending time with her people or anything, just to the point that he declined every invitation that she extended to hang out at her mom's house. Zino could already tell she was getting way too comfortable with that, and he didn't want to give her the wrong idea.

Zino looked at the clock on his dashboard just as his phone began to vibrate in his pocket. He pulled it out to see Lonnie's name flashing across it. He'd figured it was going to be her before he even looked at the screen. She called him every day when she got off work. It was like clockwork. Before she clocked in, on her break, and when she got off. She was also good for at least an hour worth of texts throughout the day.

"Hey, Zino, how are you my love?" She sounded just as chipper as she had when he'd talked to her on her break earlier.

"I'm good, Lonnie, what's good? You off?"

"Yep. You on your way to come get me?"

Zino smirked at her assertiveness. "Who told you I was coming to get you?"

"I did. I'm outside now waiting on you."

Zino looked toward the entrance of the hospital when he turned into the parking lot. "I know. I see you."

Even though he tried to fight it off as much as he could, Lonnie wasn't the only one who had fallen into their routine. He dropped her off and picked her up on most days. Occasionally skipping a morning, depending on what kind of work he'd had to do the night before.

"See, I knew you wouldn't let me down." Lonnie was smiling when he pulled up to where she was standing.

He watched her hang up before getting into the passenger seat of his car. She was smiling hard as hell, as she always did when she saw him, while buckling her seatbelt. When she finished, she leaned over the console and puckered her lips up.

"Come on, baby, give me a kiss," she said playfully.

"Man, get your ass out of here with that shit unless you ready to get this dick too."

Lonnie sucked her teeth. "You get on my nerves. You always trying to make everything nasty."

Zino shrugged. "Ain't no trying in it. I'm nasty, so the shit I say is going to be nasty too."

Lonnie rolled her eyes and sat back in her seat. She situated herself some before picking up his Walmart bag from the floor. Zino watched her dig through it like it belonged to her before pulling the candy from the bag. She flipped the bag around a few times, examining it before holding it up and looking at him.

"You don't like chocolate."

Zino gave her a nonchalant look and shrugged. "Don't you think I know that shit?"

65

"Well, what you buying chocolate for then, nigga?" She turned

to the side in her seat so she could fully see his face.

Zino honestly thought the whole show she was trying to put on

was comical. She had been doing little shit like that a lot lately. One

minute she would be laughing and playing, and the next she would

be trying to check him like she was his girlfriend.

Had she been anybody else, he probably would have ignored

her ass and cut her off after the first time, but not Lonnie. He liked

her and actually liked when she acted up about him. Though he

wasn't into the relationship thing just yet, he was still happy to have

someone who cared for him enough to show some type of emotion

on his behalf.

"Zino, I said why you got this bag of chocolate candy if you

don't eat it?" She tossed the candy at him. "You buying candy for

other girls or something?"

Lonnie pushed the side of his face with the palm of her hand

when he began to chuckle at the things she was saying.

"Oh, I see you think something is funny. Okay watch this." She snatched the bag of candy open and started eating it.

Zino looked over at her every so often smirking and shaking his head. To fuck with her, he reached for the candy like he was trying to take it out of her hand.

"Aye, put my shit back, girl."

Lonnie snatched away from him, spilling nearly the whole bag all over the front seat and floor.

"Nope, move." She swatted at the hand he'd just tried to take the candy from her with. "You want to buy candy for other females for Valentine's Day and stuff, but want to keep friend zoning me. I got something for your ungrateful ass." She tore open another piece of candy. "Tell that bitch I ate her candy." She smacked loudly. "She won't be getting this shit today, and if I find out you went and bought some more, I'ma beat your black ass."

Zino could hardly contain the laughter spilling from his mouth.

"Man, stop eating up my shit, Lonnie. I'm not playing with you." He slapped at the piece she was about to put in her mouth, hitting her bottom lip in the process.

"Oh, nigga!" Lonnie spun around again so that she was facing him. "This bitch got you putting your hands on me now?" she asked with a shocked expression. "Oh, she must be a bad one, honey," she said sarcastically. "Kudos to that hoe." Lonnie clapped as she shook her head from side to side.

"Do you see yourself right now?" Zino was still smiling as he drove. "You over there acting an ass for nothing. My hand barely touched your ass."

"It hit my whole damn lip, Zino, don't try to soften it up now. Your new hoe got you not giving a fuck about me." She pushed all the candy from her lap and looked out the window.

Zino chuckled as he watched her. "Oh, so you mad for real now, huh?"

She said nothing. Just kept looking out of the window.

"Lonnie," he sang her name playfully.

"Fuck you."

He almost swerved off the road when she said that. Lonnie cursed here and there, but she had never been the type to swear too hard. For her to be mad enough to just cuss him out had him past tickled. He even had to hold his stomach as he laughed at her.

"I'm glad you think this is funny." She smacked her teeth. "I want you to keep right on laughing when I be out here in these streets letting another nigga buy me candy and slapping your ass around for saying something about it."

"Man, I ain't even hit you that hard. You making it seem like I knuckled up and just sucker punched your ass."

"Might as well had." She touched her bottom lip. "I think my lip is starting to swell, as hard as you hit me."

Zino was laughing again when he put his hand on her thigh.

69

Their current situation was one of the main reasons he had to fuck with her. She was his solace. Always making his day brighter, even when she was fucking around.

"Man, I ain't fucking with your ass. I barely touched your damn mouth. Had you not been all in my shit, I would have never hit you any damn way." He scooted down some in his seat. "You did that shit to yourself."

Lonnie finally looked back at him. This time with a shocked expression. "Oh, she must have some good ass too, huh? You just showing all out over me today." She crossed her arms over her chest. "Take me home."

"You think I ain't? You acting crazy as fuck. I'm about to hurry up and drop your ass off."

"You know what? Nah. I'm staying with you. You won't drop me off so you can go get that hoe some more candy and lay up with her chocolate eating ass." She sucked her teeth as she sat quietly for a minute. "And I don't see how you fucking with a hoe that eat

70

something you don't eat anyway? When y'all kiss, because I know you're going to kiss the hoe because that's what you like to do, chocolate gon' be all in her teeth and shit. Fake ass. Apparently, you do like chocolate." Lonnie fumed with her arms still folded across her chest.

Zino sped the car up playfully. "Let me hurry up and get your crazy ass out of my car."

"Nigga don't speed up trying to kill me so you can be with your chocolate eating hoe." She ran her hand through her hair. "You can have the hoe. You ain't got to kill me to do that."

"Lonnie, your ass is really psycho, you know that, right?"

"Oh, now I'm psycho? This hoe must be some damn body because I'm usually funny, or silly, or I brighten your day and stuff, but today I'm psycho." She nodded. "You know what, just take me home before I kill you."

Loud laughter erupted from Zino's mouth as he stopped at the red light. "Give me a kiss, Lonnie." He leaned over the armrest

trying to kiss her face, but she swatted him away continuously. Zino

grabbed her face and turned it so that her mouth was close enough

for him to kiss it. "Man, give me some love girl and stop cutting up."

"I don't want your mouth on me. You probably just pulled it off

that chocolate eating hoe."

"Well, you just finished eating the candy I bought for her, so

wouldn't that make you a chocolate eating hoe too?"

Lonnie snatched out of his grasp and slapped him hard across

his face. "Yeah, take me to the house because I'm two seconds from

killing you. This bitch got you all kinds of brand new today, hitting

on me, calling me out my name. I just can't take it." She shook her

head and looked straight ahead. "Go, nigga! The light is green."

Zino sat back, still laughing. He'd known calling her a hoe was

going to rile her up, which was why he'd done it. He would have

never disrespected Lonnie like that, but the way she was acting right

then had him cracking the hell up. He wasn't ready for it to end just yet.

"When you see your new lil hoe, tell that bitch I salute her muthafucking ass. She's got to be some kind of bitch."

"Lonnie, all this about a bag of Snickers? For real?"

"Yes, for real. You don't eat the shit so I'm assuming it was somebody else. Your friend Uzoma ain't never here no more, so I know it ain't for him," Lonnie fussed as she unbuckled her seatbelt.

They had just pulled up to her apartment. Zino hurried to hop out of the car behind her before she could get into the house and lock him out. She was moving so fast when she got out that he ended up getting to the door just after she had opened it. Lonnie was just about to close the door in his face when he stuck his foot in the door.

"Stop playing, man." He pushed the door open and she stumbled backward.

Once he was inside, he kicked the door closed behind him and locked it before following her down the hallway. He'd been over so many times, he was practically at home there now. When he got to the back, she was fumbling through her dresser drawers.

"What you looking for clothes for?"

"So I can have my nigga come pick me up."

"Don't play with me, Lonnie." Zino chuckled, even though he found absolutely nothing about her comment funny.

"I ain't playing. I'm about to have somebody who wants me to be their Valentine to come and buy me some candy." She stood up and tossed the long-sleeved crop top onto the bed.

Zino's face frowned up when he noticed the shirt would show her stomach. Without even asking her, he snatched it from the bed and held it up, eyeing it disapprovingly.

"The hell you think you wearing this shit to?"

Lonnie looked at him over her shoulder as she walked to her closet. "To see my man."

Zino raised his eyebrows. "Oh, that's what you think, huh?" He nodded slowly to himself before walking out of the room.

He walked to the kitchen and snatched the large blue scissors from the drawer next to her refrigerator and walked back into her room. She was still shuffling through her closet, he assumed looking for some pants to wear with the shirt she thought she was about to wear.

If Lonnie thought Zino was one of these chumps that she was used to fucking with, he was surely about to show her different. He took the scissors and cut straight down the middle of her shirt.

"Lonnie," he called her name so she would turn around. "You think you about to wear this shit somewhere? Then try me." He cut some more of the shirt and threw it at her since she still hadn't turned around.

The piece of fabric flew right over her shoulder and fell to the floor. After bending down to pick it up, she spun around rapidly and caught sight of him destroying her shirt.

"Zinooooo," she yelled. "Why you cutting up my clothes?"

"Because you ain't gon' toss no lil shit like this in my face talking about another nigga and think I won't handle your ass."

Lonnie stood in disbelief as he finished cutting up her shirt. By the time he finished cutting it up the shirt was nothing more than a pile of shreds. Nobody would have ever known it was a shirt by the way he'd chopped it up.

When he finished, he kicked the pile of fabric around the floor and tossed the scissors on the dresser. "Now play with me if you want to."

Lonnie's eyes were on her shirt as he spoke. "I can't believe your retarded ass just cut up my shirt."

"Believe it." Zino walked around to where she was and stood in her face. "Now what was that you was saying about finding you another valentine?" He leaned closer into her face. "Because believe me when I tell you, I will cut his ass up the same way I did that fucking shirt. I'm not the one to bullshit with, Lonnie."

His voice was devoid of any amusement. She needed to know how serious he was. He didn't give a fuck if he'd started out joking or not, thinking about her and another man had angered him for real. He wasn't having that shit, and if she tried it, he would make good on his threat and that nigga would end up in just as many pieces as that damn shirt. He'd done it before and would do it again.

Lonnie's breathing quieted as he stood in front of her, staring at her and waiting for her to say something. Her face held a nervous expression as she twisted her mouth to the side and bit the inside of her cheek.

"You hear me?" He grabbed her side and pulled her small body to him with just enough force.

She bumped into him lightly before finding her footing again. His hand was still on her when she looked up at him with her eyebrows frowned up.

"Why you acting like this?" she asked quietly.

"Because I'm a crazy ass nigga, and you trying me."

She looked to the side, still biting on the inside of her cheek. "I don't even have another nigga."

"Better not." His dreads were falling down around his shoulders and near her face.

"It's not fair, Zino. You have all these women."

"What women, Lonnie?" He let her go and took a seat on the side of the bed. "That candy was for your psycho ass."

She looked over at him as she backed up until she was leaning against the wall. Her room was quiet as they stared at one another. Before long, she was smiling, then laughing. She laughed for a few minutes with him watching her. With his arm resting on his knee and his chin in his palm, he stared at her, not moved in the least by her laughter.

Zino was going to let her have her moment, but he needed a

little more time. He had actually allowed himself to get angry about her and anther nigga while he cut up her shirt. It was going to take him some time to get himself back together after that. His anger wasn't something that dissipated quickly.

"Why you ain't just tell me that instead of letting me act like a fool?"

He shrugged. "That was your business. I ain't tell you to assume I bought that candy for somebody else. You did all of that on your own. Common sense should have told your ass that it was for you."

"How? You ain't said nothing about Valentine's Day, and I get in your car and you got a bag of candy. What was I supposed to think?"

Zino sat up and leaned back on her bed. He posted up on his elbows so he could still see her. "You should have at least thought that I would have bought you more than that little bag of candy if you was my Valentine. I just picked that shit up for you because I was at the store and I knew I was about to come scoop you."

79

Lonnie's face smile beamed bright. "Aww, so you were thinking about me at the store?" she squealed playfully. "So, I get just because gifts from you now?"

Zino hadn't looked at it like that, but now that she'd put it that way, he guessed she did. "If that's how you want to put it."

Lonnie launched onto him out of nowhere. Her body landed roughly on top of his, knocking some of the wind out of him. He took a deep breath, trying to gather himself as she straddled his lap, positioning herself right on his dick. She was smiling down at him as she played with his stomach.

"Lonnie, get off of me before you make my dick hard."

Her eyes rolled dramatically. "Why do you always do that?"

"I just tell the truth. Now get your ass down."

Instead of getting down, Lonnie leaned forward and tried to kiss his lips, but he turned his head. "Go head on, now. I just told you."

She was giggling into his neck when he pushed her head away

from his face playfully. "Just one kiss?"

Zino knew that was a bad idea because he hadn't had sex in almost three weeks. He had really been trying to chill until Lonnie decided to bust it open, but she was making that shit hard as hell. He hadn't thought it would take her this long to get with the program. She wasn't budging, but always wanted to do shit like that to make his dick hard.

"One kiss, Zino." She pecked the side of his mouth. "One." She kissed the center of his neck where his Adam's apple was. "One… Zino… just one." She licked up the side of his neck and kissed where her tongue stopped.

Zino lay beneath her, letting her do her thing. He was more than positive once she felt that hard dick poking her little ass, she would stop all that playing. He could already feel it rising, so surely in the next few minutes she would too.

Lonnie kissed his neck again, this time with her tongue, even sucking it a little.

"You smell so good," she moaned after inhaling his scent.

"You feel my dick, don't you?"

She looked down at him and smiled as she nodded her head.

"Then either take them panties off and let me get me some or get your ass off me."

Lonnie had still been kissing his neck, but stopped once she started laughing. Just like he'd figured she would, Lonnie pushed herself from his body. Her body dragging against his didn't make anything any better, especially when her face stopped directly at his midsection.

Zino didn't understand why she wanted to tease him like that, but he watched her anyway. Lonnie looked down at the swollen bulge in his pants and licked her lips before looking back up at him. Surprising him the most, she ran her hand over it and picked it up.

Her small hand wrapped around him and stroked up and down the best she could through his sweat pants. Zino watched her as his breathing sped up. Her face was serious as she watched her hand fondle him. She looked so sexy, it made him think about how she would look if they were naked and she was doing that same shit.

"Let my dick go, Lonnie," he told her as he sat up. "You ain't finna' give me blue balls because you want to fuck around.

She looked up at him before placing a quick hard kiss on the part of his dick that was the closest to her mouth, and standing from the bed.

"I should make you give me some pussy after that shit right there."

She winked at him. "I will, soon."

Zino let out a frustrated breath. "What the fuck we waiting on?"

When Lonnie started laughing, he could tell she heard the confusion and exasperation in his voice. He'd heard it too, but fuck it. He needed some pussy, and she needed to be the one to give it to him.

"What you about to do?"

Zino shook his head, but didn't say anything. He didn't have anything planned other than chilling with her to be for real. He'd worked all night with Brasi and Kindo, so he was taking the day off to relax.

"Well, my mama is cooking if you want to go over there."

Here we go.

"Nah, I think I'ma chill. You can go, though. Just hit me up when you leave."

Lonnie instantly began to pout and beg him to come. Zino told her no continuously, but for some reason he ended up giving in. He didn't know if it was because he was tired of her always begging or the mention of cabbage and fried chicken that had him changing his mind. It really didn't matter which one it was because they both led him to her mother's house.

Chapter 4: I don't want to go back there

Since Zino had officially set himself up, he sat patiently on the bed waiting for Lonnie to get herself ready to leave. She had a list of things she needed to do, and was taking forever to do it all. Once she finally finished changing her clothes, they left and headed to her mom's house.

Zino hoped all the way there that it wouldn't be a house full of people. Apparently, God had been on his side that one time because there were no cars in the yard other than her mother's red Camry.

When he and Lonnie got inside, her mother jumped up to fix him a plate. She took a seat across from him and Lonnie and watched them as they ate. The smile on her face was warm and put him at ease whenever he did end up making eye contact with her.

"How've you been Zino, baby?" Her hands were clasped

together beneath her chin as she sat watching him and Lonnie eat.

"Fine, ma'am," he told her. "Yourself?"

"Blessed." She was still smiling when she looked over at Lonnie. "I've been telling miss thing here to bring you back over."

"I told you I always invite him, Mama. He just never wants to come." She bit her chicken. "He's crazy."

Zino looked over at her and smirked when she opened her mouth to show him her chewed up food.

"Zino, if you're going to be Lonnie's boyfriend, don't you think you're going to hang out with her family at some point?"

"This nigga ain't my boyfriend, Ma," Lonnie told her with a mouth full of food. "He ain't even asked me to be his valentine yet."

Her mother gasped and looked at Zino with her mouth ajar. "Now, Zino, I know you're too sweet for these lies that Lonnie are telling to be true."

Zino's nose twitched as he tried to fight back the smirk that was rising across his face. "Lonnie is a liar. I bought her a bag of candy today to ask her, and she spazzed out on me. She threw candy all around my car and everything."

Lonnie and her mother both laughed at his comment. Lonnie then went on to tell her mother about how Zino hadn't told her the candy was hers until she'd started acting a fool. She and Zino went back and forth for a while, trying to make her mother believe them.

All she did was laugh and shake her head at their playful bickering. When Zino was finished eating, she excused herself from the table and made him another plate. She even refilled his glass of juice. Zino wished for a second that this was something he could get used to.

Having a family seemed to be cool, especially the mother part. He had been missing that for years, and Lonnie's mom always made him think about it. That was one of the main reasons he turned down almost every invitation to her mom's house. He didn't like to think about that kind of stuff. It put him too far in his feelings.

"Zino, you okay?" she asked him, interrupting his thoughts.

He looked up at her with a mouth full of cornbread and cabbage. Because he couldn't deny the fact that he had actually been thinking about his mother, he couldn't mask the expression on his face.

"Yes ma'am, I'm fine," he tried to convince her.

She tilted her head to the side. "You sure? You looked like something was on your mind just then." She reached across the table and patted his hand softly. "Tell me about it."

"Ma, leave him alone," Lonnie intervened.

"You leave me alone and eat your food." She patted Zino's hand again. "I'm not bothering you, am I, baby?"

Though she really was bothering him, Zino lied. "No ma'am."

She smiled. "Now tell me, baby. Tell me what troubles you. I know it's something." She waited for him to answer. "You don't have to tell me in front of Lonnie if you don't want to. I can make her get out."

Zino and Lonnie both laughed at her before Lonnie spoke. "Don't do me because I'll leave. I don't want to hear you play counselor anyway." Lonnie stood. "Always trying to fix somebody." She chuckled as she disappeared into the kitchen.

As soon as she was gone, her mother looked back at Zino. He assumed she was waiting for him to tell her something, but he honestly didn't know what she wanted to hear. There was so much stuff he could tell her, but that would take all day, and he was more than sure she didn't want to hear all of that anyway.

If he told her half of his real life, she'd been telling Lonnie to run. Hell, she might even put him out of her house right then.

"Lonnie told me that you had a brother that passed?"

"Oh Lord," Zino heard Lonnie say from the kitchen.

He tittered a little before nodding his head. "I actually had two brothers to pass."

She covered her chest and gave him a sympathetic look. "Were you all your mother's only children?"

Zino cleared his throat. "None of us shared a mom."

She nodded and looked at him to keep going, but he didn't.

"So, how was your Christmas?"

"Fine."

"Y'all ain't talking about nothing. I can come back in here." Lonnie sat back in her seat with a plate of peach cobbler.

Zino looked over at her before taking her plate, fork and all, and eating her dessert. She slapped his shoulder before getting up and going back into the kitchen to get herself some more. When she came back, he was already almost finished with what she'd had on the plate.

"Lonnie, just bring the whole thing in here."

Lonnie did as she was told and sat the pan of peach cobbler in the center of the table. As soon as she did, her mother pushed it toward Zino.

"Eat as much as you want, baby."

"You ain't tell me to eat as much as I wanted," Lonnie told her.

Zino looked over and winked at her. "Stop being jealous, lil girl."

Lonnie rolled her eyes before going back to eating her pie.

"Zino, you didn't tell me how your Christmas was. I mean, since I guess you were too good to spend it with us."

"No ma'am, it wasn't like that. I just didn't want to intrude. I was okay chilling at the house."

"At the house? You was at home by yourself on Christmas?" Lonnie asked him

He'd told her he had gone to Columbus with Uzoma. Zino had

91

totally forgotten all about that. So, versus lying and going too far into an explanation, he just nodded his head.

"Christmas is all about family, Zino. You should have at least spent time with yours," Lonnie's mother said.

"Don't have one." Zino hoped that would end the conversation, but he was wrong.

Lonnie began asking all kinds of questions until her mother told her to stop. Zino had just finished his pie and dug into the pan to get more. He sat and ate as Lonnie and her mother went back and forth about him telling them about his past. Her mother insisted that they didn't pry, while Lonnie, on the other hand, wanted to know.

"It's cool," he told her mother. "My mother left me when I was young. I'm over it now. I have a sister that lives in Virginia with her own little family, and an uncle in jail. We used to be close, but once I went to jail, all of that changed, and now we don't talk anymore." Zino decided to just put it all out there, that way they would stop asking questions, and her mother would stop probing him every time he came around.

"You don't miss them?" Lonnie rubbed his shoulder softly.

Zino shrugged.

"I think you should reach out to them. Everybody needs somebody."

"I got you, right?" he asked her.

"Yeah, but still…"

"Family is still a good thing to have, Zino," her mother chimed in.

"Maybe," he told them before finishing his pie.

He was more than happy that they decided to let the subject go. Neither of them said anything else about it. They'd even switched the conversation to something else, even though that wasn't anything he wanted to talk about either.

They were all supposed to meet at her cousin Tasha's gravesite within the next few minutes to release balloons for her birthday. Zino groaned inwardly because he most definitely was not up for no shit like that. All he could think about was how he should have followed his first mind and told Lonnie no when she asked him about her mother's house. Now, once again, he'd set himself up to be in the middle of some shit he wanted no parts of.

"It's not going to take long, I promise," Lonnie told him as they stood on her mother's porch.

They'd finished eating and excused themselves while her mother got herself ready to go.

"Man, nah, Lonnie. I ain't with no graveyards, especially if your people gone be there crying and shit."

"Please, Zino. I want you to be there with me."

Lonnie wrapped both of her arms around his waist as she looked up at him, trying to change his mind. Zino knew in the back of his

94

mind he should have told her ass no, but all he felt was himself shaking his head up and down.

"Thank you." She kissed the bottom of his chin. "If it gets to be too much, we can leave."

Zino nodded, but didn't say anything because if that was the case, then why were they even going? He didn't need anyone to tell him that it was going to get out of hand. It was the girl's birthday, and instead of being out celebrating it like they should have been, they were going to her grave.

That thought alone was damn near too much. Actually, being there and seeing her name on the stone and releasing balloons into the air and shit was definitely about to stir up too many emotions. He hated that he had even agreed to go.

Lonnie had better be glad that he knew she was probably going to be sad as hell and crying and shit, and he didn't want her to go through that alone. He'd seen firsthand how her cousin's death had affected her in the beginning. He was no fool to think that she had

95

gotten over it that fast, and if he didn't know anything else, he knew grieving alone was a muthafucka. That shit hurt even worse, it seemed.

After her mother finally emerged from the house, they all got into their cars and left. Zino took one deep breath after the next, trying to prepare himself for what he was about to do. Just seeing the large flower that Lonnie's mom had was enough to get his emotions going.

The graveyard wasn't too far from the house, so they were parking next to what he assumed to be her other family members' cars within minutes. Lonnie grabbed his hand the moment they were out of the car and following her mother through the other graves.

Zino looked straight ahead, trying his hardest not to look at any of the names or pictures on the graves. He could feel himself getting worked up, and he wanted to hold it together the best he could for Lonnie. She was sad for her own self, he didn't want her trying to cater to him again if he got too wrapped up in his feelings.

"There they go, ma," Lonnie pointed at the people standing around another grave with balloons and flowers in their hands.

Zino's heart beat faster and faster the closer they got to her family. By the time they were next to all of the other people, Zino could barely breathe. Some were already crying, while others looked like they were on the verge of it.

Graveyards had been off limits for him from the day he buried Harper. That was still one of the worst days of his life. He had grown to love him like the father he never had, so his passing had been very tough. Not to mention the fact that since he was gone, it meant that Zino was alone in the world. That feeling alone was enough to send him over the edge.

He still remembered that day as if it had just happened. It was dark and raining like crazy. Harper's funeral was pretty packed since he had been well known in the hood. Zino had seen the majority of the people there around town when making deliveries for Harper, but there was only one who stood out amongst the crowd.

It was dark and sunken in in certain spots. The color was a lot ashier than he remembered, and her eye sockets resembled that of a skeleton's. Along with her face, her body was just as worn out. It was barely there, nothing more than skin and bones covered in tattered dirty clothing.

Zino stared at his mother with so much pain circulating through his heart that he couldn't understand why it hadn't broken yet. Surely a pain that excruciating should have broken it to pieces. She looked like walking death, and there was nothing he could do about it.

Gone was the lady he'd known as his mother. She'd been replaced by a drug addicted street walker. It pained Zino to no end to watch people turn their noses up at her and push her around and away from them as she made her way to Harper's casket.

She was nothing more than a common dope fiend, and they were treating her as such, so he couldn't be mad with them. Instead, he stood on the front row of the chairs watching in defeat. Once she finally made it to the casket to see Harper lying there, shit really went bad.

The way she screamed and hollered, one would have thought he was her man and not her dealer. She screamed obscenities about coming back to her and how much she loved him and shit until one of Harper's goons, who Zino knew as Tommy, grabbed her and tried to pull her from the body.

She kicked and screamed like a mad woman until Zino jumped up to grab her from him. He couldn't take the way people were looking at her. She fought against him just as hard until she realized who he was. She then began hugging onto his neck and apologizing for leaving him. A bunch of shit Zino wasn't interested in hearing. He carried her away from the gravesite and stood her to her feet. Once she was upright, he told her he loved her before turning to walk away.

I didn't leave you, Zino. I loved you, but I couldn't take care of you then, so I let him have you... he's your father, Zino.

That was the last thing Zino ever heard come out of his mother's mouth. He hadn't seen or heard from her again after that. He'd wanted to turn around and ask her about what she'd just told him right then, but it wasn't time. He'd had enough of her embarrassing herself for one day. He didn't want to see any more of it.

He found out later on that night from Tommy that what she said had indeed been true. She'd gotten addicted to drugs, and Harper had been threatening to take Zino from her if she didn't clean herself up. When she didn't, he made good on his word.

Zino was wounded even deeper after finding out the truth, but there was no point in crying over spilled milk. His father was dead, and his mother might as well had been too. From that day to this one he had hated graveyards.

The loud shriek that sounded off next to him brought Zino's eyes from the sky. He had been staring at the birds flying past to keep his eyes off the tombstones, but hearing Lonnie yell like that got his attention. When he looked at her she was crawling on her hands and knees toward her cousin's headstone.

Though Zino was battling his own demons, Lonnie quickly became his first priority. Without thinking, he reached to grab her from the ground. He picked her small body up with ease as she lay back limply in his arms.

"Stop it, Lonnie. You're going to be sick if you keep crying like this," he whispered into her ear.

"I... I... I just miss her so much," she cried as she tried to get back to the ground.

"Just hold her, baby," Lonnie's mother told him.

Zino looked at her and nodded his head. He stepped back, still holding her in his arms. Flashes of him holding his mother at Harper's funeral zoomed through his mind, but he shook them away. He'd had to carry her away the same way he was doing Lonnie right then.

"No! No, let me go back, Zino. Please let me just go back I need

101

to talk to her." She cried.

Her sobs were so loud and strong, it was as if Zino could feel her pain through them. She was laid out in his arms wailing uncontrollably. Zino was doing all that he could to hold her, but she was fighting to get away. She was fighting to get out of his arms so hard that he tripped over someone else's flowers and lost his balance.

He and Lonnie fell to the ground with more impact than expected but he recovered quickly and steadied them. Once he was firm in his spot on the ground he was able to hold her a little better. Her body was between his legs as he held her from behind.

Her head lay back against his shoulder as she cried into his neck. "I miss her." She sniffed hard. "I don't know why they took her from me," she whined.

Zino nodded his head as he listened to her. "I know, baby. I know you miss her." He kissed her forehead.

"I don't know what to do, Zino." She sighed as she snuggled closer to him.

Zino squeezed her body as close to him as he could and kissed all over her forehead as he thought about his own family. On most days, he didn't know what to do either. He'd lost so many loved ones, he didn't know either.

"It hurts so badddd," she cried some more. "I just want her back."

His mother's touch, Harper's fatherly concern, Tek's laugh, and Tone's voice all flashed through Zino's mind at once. It was like a movie playing back to back as he listened to her crying words. Zino rocked back and forth in an effort to calm down what he felt rising, but he couldn't.

Everything going on around him right then took him to every moment he'd ever had with either of them, and before he could stop them, his eyes began to water. His throat was tight and his body was starting to shake. Everything in him was starting feel numb as he

103

listened to Lonnie's weeping.

"Zinooo," She whimpered into his chest.

He looked down at her face that was covered in tears. She was looking to him to make her feel better, but he had nothing. There was no way he could do that for her right then. He couldn't even control his own feelings. Looking into her eyes while she was experiencing so much pain did absolutely nothing for him except make him think of Phoenix the day Tone was murdered.

The pain in Lonnie's eyes and cries were an exact duplication of Phoenix's that day. She had been screaming and hollering that exact same way as she lay over his dead body. He'd thought that was the hardest things he'd ever had to see, but looking at Lonnie was most definitely a close second.

"It' gon' be alright, Lonnie." He kissed her mouth. "I got you, baby." He rocked her a little harder to assure he was there.

She held onto his shirt as she sniffed silently. In the distance,

Zino could see her family releasing the balloons. They floated higher and higher. Further and further away, out of the grasp of everyone who had let them go. Much like their family member.

"Fuck, man!" Zino groaned as water began to spill down his face.

He sniffed as hard as he could to stop his tears, but nothing worked. When he couldn't contain himself anymore, he tried to push away from Lonnie. When she noticed that he was now the one that needed comforting, she hopped up and wrapped her arms around his neck. She kneeled in front of him, holding his head to her bosom as he fought his true feelings.

"I've got to go, Lon." He pulled himself from her grasp and stood up.

"Let me go with you." She ran after him once he began to walk away.

"No. Go with your family. I'll be straight." He pushed her away from him with a little more force this time as he headed toward the car.

His tears were pouring from his face, racking his body by then. He'd barely been able to get his words out, but he didn't want her to see him like that. He really hated right then that he'd even agreed to go out there with her. The feeling of being alone and missing his people hadn't surfaced like that... ever.

Zino barely made it to the car before he bent over, resting his hands on his knees. His sobs had taken over so much that he couldn't even stand.

"Zino," Lonnie's mother's voice came from behind him. "Come here, baby." She grabbed onto his arm making him stand up.

He was much taller than her, so when she pulled him to her for a hug, he had to bend over to be comforted. She held him tightly in her arms and allowed him to cry on her shoulder. Being in her arms felt so much different than being in Lonnie's.

106

Even with Lonnie trying as hard as she could to comfort him, it hadn't worked. Being held by her mother was something so different. It was so warm and loving. He'd had that once, a long time ago. So long ago that he didn't really remember how it felt until he'd felt it again.

"It's going to be okay, baby. Just let it all out." She patted his back and continued talking to him as he cried.

Once Zino finally let go of the hold he'd placed on himself, he cried for what felt like hours. Lonnie's mom held him the entire time. By the time he finished and she released him, he felt utterly drained. He had nothing left in him at the moment. That agonizing pain had taken every ounce of energy he'd had.

"We're going to talk, okay?" She patted his face as she looked into his eyes.

"Yes, ma'am."

"You go home and get you some rest, okay?"

He nodded. "I…" He sighed. "I just don't know what to do." His voice sounded just as drained as he felt.

"You have to move on, Zino. I know it hurts, baby, but life must go on. You can't keep harboring all of this pain like this. You have to let go." She rubbed his face softly. "It's okay to miss them and still move on."

Zino nodded and wiped his face with the back of his hand. She looked at him for a little while longer before pulling him to her for one more hug and letting him go. When she moved, he saw Lonnie standing behind her.

Her face looked just as tired as he assumed his probably did. Her mother gave her a long hug as well before walking away. Once she was gone, Zino and Lonnie stood looking at one another for a minute until he reached his hand out to her.

She walked to him in a hurry. When she was in front of him, he grabbed her hand held her in his arms. He picked her up from the ground so that he could hold her close to him. His nose ran along her neck as she squeezed her arms around his neck. He kissed her ear, then her neck, before finally landing his lips on top of her.

When he pulled away, he pecked her nose before placing her back down on her feet. "Thank you for making me come here with you today."

She didn't say anything, just looked at him.

"You ready to go?"

This time, she nodded.

"Cool, let's go," he told her as she rounded the car, headed for the passenger side.

Once she got in, he backed out of the parking lot and got onto the highway headed to her spot. He didn't know if it was because they were both too tired from all the crying they'd done or they just didn't have anything to say, but the ride to her apartment was a quiet one.

"You staying here with me tonight?" she asked him once they'd gotten to her place and were at the door.

"You want me to?"

"Would I have asked if I didn't." She smirked at him.

"Well, I guess I'm staying then, but don't be trying to sleep with your lil ass all up on me either."

Lonnie's giggle was like the sunshine on his very cloudy day right then. "Nigga, you wish I would put this ass on you."

Zino pushed his way through her door, and grabbed a handful of her butt as he passed her. "I damn sure do. You need to stop acting so stingy with that shit." He pulled his jacket off and plopped down on the sofa. "It probably ain't all that anyway."

Again, her giggle eased more of his pain. "If it ain't that good, why you begging for it then?"

"Because I ain't got shit else to do." He looked at her with a broad smile on his face. "Plus, I heard skinny girls got that water for your ass. Niggas be saying that shit be wet as fuck."

"You ain't heard that mess from nowhere."

Zino chuckled as he rested his hand on her thigh. "I swear I heard it."

Lonnie shook her head at him. "Well, I can't speak for other girls, but I know mine be wet."

Zino kicked his shoes off and looked over at her. "Let me see then."

The room was quiet as they participated in a silent staring contest. He licked his lips as he looked from her face down to her breasts, then to her legs, which were gapped open due to the way she was sitting. Zino knew Lonnie liked to act all shy and shit, so instead of saying anything else, he took it upon himself to reach over and stroke her through her pants.

She tried to close her legs at first, but he shook his head from side to side and tapped the inside of her thigh.

"Nah, open 'em back up." He referred to her legs.

111

She stared at him for a long time before opening her legs back up. Zino went all in this time and began to unbutton her pants. When she lifted up for him to pull them off, he got excited. As she sat in front of him in nothing but her jacket and panties, Zino picked her up and sat her on his lap.

He removed her jacket, shirt, then her bra. Once she sat exposed on his lap, he ran his fingertips down her back before grabbing her face and kissing her mouth. Lonnie kissed him back with just as much as aggression as he was giving her.

"Wrap your legs around me," he told her as he stood from the sofa.

Lonnie did as she was told, and he carried her from the living room to the bathroom. He flipped the shower on while still holding her, and waited for the water to warm up before putting her back onto her feet.

"Take your panties and socks off, and get in."

Once again, Lonnie did as she was told as she watched him undress in front of her. Her eyes went from the long black locs that fell around his neck and shoulders to the sculpted torso and arms. She gasped and widened her eyes when he removed his jeans and boxers.

"Now, Zino…" she said in a skeptical tone.

He grabbed her naked body as he took a seat on the side of the tub. "Don't get scared now." He ran his hands all over her sides and down her butt to the back of her thighs.

He placed kisses all over her stomach, licking and sucking in certain places. Lonnie shivered every time he touched her, and it was making him hornier by the second. Even with her having been at work all day, then out in the open air at the cemetery, she still smelled good.

When he couldn't take it anymore, Zino stood up and pushed the shower curtain back before grabbing her and pulling them both into the tub. The water from the shower cascaded down over his

113

back as he pushed her against the wall and picked her back up.

Her legs and arms went around his neck and waist immediately. She grinded her body against his subtly as he kissed her neck and massaged her butt in both palms of his hands. Her body felt so good in his hands that he didn't see how he'd waited that long to feel her.

"You know I've been waiting for you, right?" He bit the soft skin just above her breast before licking around her nipple.

"For how long?" She moaned.

"For about three weeks."

She snickered first before he followed. "You me sick. Three weeks ain't shit."

He let her nipple go to look at her face. "For a nigga like me it is." He hoisted her up some more so that he could find her opening.

"You're such a thot, Zino."

He slid the head of his dick around her pussy stopping any more talking that she thought she was about to do.

"You're about to see why." He pressed her back into the wall and pushed his way deep into her tight tunnel. "Gotdamn girl," he cursed. "You must ain't been letting nobody fuck you. Your pussy tight as hell."

Lonnie was clearly in too much pain to talk back because all she did was lay her forehead against his shoulder.

"Oh shit, I dun' finally found a way to shut your ass up, huh?" He boasted as he forced himself deeper inside of her.

It took a few seconds for him to get in and get comfortable enough to move, and when he did, he grunted roughly into her ear. His arms flexed with her every stroke he delivered. Unlike all the other women he was used to fucking, Lonnie didn't make very much noise.

If his ear hadn't been near her mouth he wouldn't have even heard the small gasps she made whenever he went too deep. The water from the shower ain't have shit on the fluids leaking down his thighs from Lonnie's body. Zino was in love. Fuck anybody who told him different.

He had been banging chicks from day to night for years, and it ain't have shit on being up in Lonnie for the few minutes he'd been loving on her.

"Sounds like," she grunted into his ear. "Sounds like I found a way to shut you up too." She was looking at him when he looked up at her.

Zino wanted to smile, but he didn't. Instead, he grabbed her lips with his and devoured them. He needed something to take his mind off the tingling in the head of his dick. He was still kissing her and stroking her body slowly when he felt her legs tighten around his back.

"Umm." She moaned a little louder than she had the entire time they'd been wrapped up into each other.

"I know you ain't about to bust that quick?" Zino licked the side of her mouth. "You about to give it to me already, Lonnie?" He coaxed along her orgasm.

Lonnie's eyes clasped shut tightly before she gasped loudly and squeezed her arms around his neck tighter. Zino's body was pressed against hers as she rode her orgasm. He watched her in awe like some kind of virgin ass nigga fucking for the first time.

Once her body went limp in his arms, he knew he was in the safe zone and allowed himself to enjoy her insides until he felt himself about to bust. He pumped only a few seconds longer before pulling out and letting himself go onto her stomach.

His body shuddered lightly, as did hers. Lonnie was still holding him tightly when he pulled back so that he could see her face. He was about to put her down, but she held him tighter.

"No, stay right there."

"Aight." He kept her in his arms, but sat down on the side of

117

the shower, letting the water run over them both.

For the first time in his entire life, Zino didn't want to leave after sex. He kissed her neck again, not sure if he ever wanted to leave her at all. Sex or not, Lonnie was making it harder and harder for him to separate from her. Maybe… just maybe… it was because this time he didn't need to.

Chapter 5: The future always looks better than the

past

The small doctor's office was packed from wall to wall with people. There were men and women everywhere. Some of them looked to be together while the others were merrily clocking in for their nine to five. There were almost just as many nurses as there were patients in the office, which was why Joc didn't understand what could have been possibly taking them so long to see her.

She had gotten to the doctor's office for her appointment nearly thirty minutes before her actual appointment time and hadn't even had her vitals taken yet. To make matters worse, she hadn't had the chance to eat breakfast that morning in an effort to make her appointment on time.

Her stomach was growling and the baby was making her so

much more nauseous than she probably would have normally been. All of it was causing her mood to sour by the second. She had been so excited talking to Uzoma about her first real appointment the night before, and the crowded office was ruining it for her.

"Is this your first time coming here?"

Joc looked to her left and saw a girl with a large gap and ugly weave talking to her. She was straining her eyes to look at the paper in Joc's hand that had been given to her upon checking in. Joc moved the paper so that she couldn't see before nodding her head.

Although Joc wasn't the friendliest person, she wasn't the meanest either, but she didn't like the girl being all in her business.

"Oh, okay. Mine too. You know what doctor you're seeing?"

"Dr. Chambers."

Her smile broadened across her face. "Me too. Maybe we'll have our baby at the same time."

Joc gave a fake smile before turning her head and looking down at her phone. She needed to do something to keep herself from rolling her eyes at the girl. She didn't even know how far along Joc was, so just how in the fuck would she just assume because they were seeing the same doctor that they were going to deliver at the same time?

Furthermore, Uzoma had made it perfectly clear that she would not be in Brooklyn upon the arrival of their child.

"I started not to even come today. After my baby daddy decided going to get his car washed was more important than checking on our child, I was pissed off," she rambled as if Joc cared.

"Girl, I feel you," Joc replied dryly.

Joc could see the girl turning in her seat so that she could look at her. "Your baby daddy didn't want to come either?"

"He's out of town. He doesn't live in Brooklyn."

"That nigga still should have came." She smacked her teeth. "He came here to get you pregnant." She flipped her hair over her shoulder. "If it was me, I would have made his ass come."

Joc's entire face frowned as she turned to look at the girl. "How?" She waited for an answer. "Please tell me just how in the fuck would you have made my baby daddy do anything when you can't even make your baby daddy leave his car alone long enough to check on your baby?"

The girl looked at Joc and rolled her eyes. "I'm not saying your baby daddy, I'm talking about if he was mine and he was out of town," she sassed as if she made any more sense than she had before.

"Again, bitch, I'ma ask you how. How the fuck was you about to do that?"

The girl's face let Joc know she didn't appreciate being called a bitch, but Joc wished she would jump stupid with her lil skinny ass. Joc could mop the whole doctor's office with her ass without even trying.

"Just forget it because you don't get it anyway."

122

"Yeah, let's just forget it." Joc turned back in her seat and finished her text to Uzoma.

"Girl, you wouldn't believe who's sitting up in here with me." A voice that Joc was very familiar with caught her attention. "My sister wife, bitch." She began giggling again.

Joc took in a deep breath. Clearly, God needed a laugh or something because he was seriously trying her. How had she run into not one but two dummies within minutes of each other? When she looked up and her eyes landed on Risha, all she could do was shake her head and look back down.

How could her day get any worse? It couldn't. She was convinced. There was not one way that her day could get any worse than it was at that moment.

"Jocelynn's ass, girl." Risha paused for a moment. "Yeah, girl, I guess Promise got both of our asses this time around." Her laughter made Joc's skin crawl.

Joc looked up at her and rolled her eyes. "Girl, stop talking about me like I won't beat your ass."

Risha giggled again before she stopped and rolled her neck at Joc. "You might as well drop that little attitude, honey. Our kids are about to be siblings now, so we might as well be friends." She burst out laughing like she had actually said something funny.

"Girl, you wish."

A sharp elbow to her arm had Joc looking to her side. The little dumb chick from before was leaning over trying to talk to her.

"Y'all got the same baby daddy?"

Joc frowned at her before looking over at Risha. "Hell fuck no."

Risha's stomach was a lot bigger than it had been the last time Joc had seen her. She looked to be about six or seven months, and that baby was kicking her ass. She looked horrible. Her face was all puffy and her nose looked like a fucking bell pepper sitting on her damn face.

Her neck was dark and her face looked like it had broken out. There were bumps every damn where. The more Joc looked at her the more disgusted she got with herself. How in the hell had she allowed Promise to cheat on her with a bitch who looked like that?

Then not only did she allow the nigga to cheat and continue getting caught, but she'd actually let him make her feel bad about herself when Risha didn't look better than the bottom of Joc's shoe. She felt so stupid for a second. She had seriously been a damn fool.

"Hey bae, our other baby mama is here," Risha said into her phone.

Just by what she'd chosen to say, Joc safely assumed that it had to have been Promise that she was talking to. Little did she know, she wouldn't have gotten pregnant by Promise with Uzoma's dick. That was the one thing she had made sure of. She had allowed him to treat her like shit, but she refused to get knocked up and the nigga treated her baby like crap too. Fuck no. She popped her pills daily with that nigga.

125

Joc was busy texting on her phone trying her best to ignore Risha and big mouth next to her when the nurse called her name. She breathed a sigh of relief and stood up. She followed the short white nurse who had just called her name.

"Hello, Jocelynn, I'm Cindy. How are you today?"

"Fine, and yourself?"

"I'm good. Do you know how far along you are today?"

Joc shook her head. "No ma'am, this is my first visit. The last time I went to a doctor all they did was take my blood to determine my pregnancy."

She patted Joc's arm. "Very well. We're going to send you over to ultrasound instead then so we can see what's going on with baby, okay?"

"Yes, ma'am."

She showed Joc back to the door they had just come in. "Have a seat back out in the waiting room and the ultrasound tech should

126

be calling you shortly."

Joc wanted to suck her teeth and complain, but instead she nodded, gave a half smile, and walked back out into the waiting room. As she was headed back to her seat, Cindy called for big mouth. She smiled and nudged Joc's arm as she walked past her.

Joc totally ignored her gesture at making friends and continued back to the seat she had been sitting in. Before she could even sit down, her nostrils were reacquainted with a smell they'd become quite familiar with. Her eyeballs rolled from top to bottom continuously as she situated herself in her seat.

"What's good, big sexy? You looking nice today."

"Fuck you, Promise," Jocelynn told him without even making eye contact.

"Big sexy? Nigga you better act like you know I'm sitting here."

Joc wanted to tell Risha that she didn't have to worry about shit Promise was saying to her, but she didn't even bother. That was their business. Promise was her problem now. She could have his disrespectful ass and everything that came with him.

"I knew the only reason your ass got out the car was because I told you she was in here."

"Aye, chill the fuck out with all that shit, B." Promise told her. "Joc, why you ain't tell me about the baby?"

Joc knew her face had to be tired of frowning because that was all she had been doing since getting to that doctor's office. For some reason, everybody wanted to get on her damn nerves.

"How far along are you?" he asked her, probably trying to determine if he was the father. "Whose baby is it because I know it ain't mine." He chuckled nervously. "Because you gon' have to give me some papers on it before I claim any muthafucking thing."

"What the fuck are you and your bitch on today? My baby does not belong to either one of y'all sorry asses. So please leave me alone."

128

Promise leaned up in his seat. "So, it ain't mine?"

Joc finally gave him her undivided attention. "My nigga, no."

"So, whose is it then?"

Risha sucked her teeth. "Why does it matter to you so much? You claim you don't fuck with the hoe no more, why it matter who's her baby daddy?"

Joc smirked at Risha's insecurity when it came to her. Clearly, Promise did her ass the same way he had been doing Joc.

"Listen to your bitch this time, Promise. This baby over here ain't got shit to do with your ass."

She smiled inwardly when she saw his facial expression. It was evident that he had really thought her baby had the possibility of being his. He was just as stupid as Risha if he thought that. She would never! Looking at him and Risha right then was one of the happiest moments of her life.

Joc was so happy to be out of that toxic love triangle that she didn't know what to do. She could have been easily sitting up in the clinic next to Risha's ass for real, arguing about Promise. All she could do was thank God for good sense because he had truly spared her with that one.

"Excuse me, I'm looking for a patient named Jocelynn." The southern African accent quieted everybody in the room.

Joc looked around the room for him. Even though she'd know that voice from anywhere, he hadn't told her that he would be coming up for the appointment. Her heart fluttered and even skipped a beat or two as she finally located the love of her life.

As always, all eyes were on him. Every woman in there that was alone, and even a few that were with their own man was looking in his direction.

"She's here for a Dr. Chambers, I think," he told the nurse.

His back was turned to Joc as he stood against the counter waiting for the receptionist to tell him where Joc was. Unlike most days, he wasn't in his causal Nike gear, today he was dressed in a pair of black Levi jeans, black Timberland boots, and a long sleeved red button up with black patches on the elbow, with the black vest she'd picked out from J. Crew.

She knew that shirt and vest because she'd nearly bust her pussy open for him in the dressing room that day at the outlet when he'd tried it on for her to see before she left Georgia. His sandy colored locs were hanging down to the middle of his back and around his shoulders. They were wavy and shiny like she liked them.

She could see his side profile and was falling deeper in love by the second. The hair on his chin and the side of his face was making her swoon every time he spoke. Joc was so caught up in her man's appearance that she hadn't even got his attention to let him know she was right behind him.

Much like every other woman in the room, she just wanted to admire his beauty. His tall frame towered over every single person in the building, making him stand out even more. Not that anybody

131

with eyes would have ever missed him.

Uzoma Youngblood. Lord! That was one fine man. Joc couldn't stop the fluttering in her stomach for nothing as she basked in the fact that he was there with her, and that a man as fine as him wanted her. On most days, that was still hard for her to believe.

"Yes sir, she's here. Dr. Chamber's waiting area is right there to the left," Joc heard the receptionist tell him.

"Thank you."

Oh goodness, and that accent! Joc closed her eyes briefly, just enjoying the thought of him. When she opened them back up he was walking toward her. He still hadn't laid eyes on her yet but he would soon if he looked hard enough.

"I know you ain't pregnant by that nigga?" Bitterness was laced all through Promise's voice. "You could have did better than that terrorist ass muthafucka. Weak ass accent."

Joc was enjoying the hate in Promise's voice. He knew Uzoma

132

was the shit, so he was trying to find any way he could to down him, but all that did was make Joc love Uzoma more.

"Hey Mr. Youngblood," Joc waved at him with the largest smile on her face. "What you doing here?" She stood up when he got to her.

Like he always did whenever she was close to him, Uzoma grabbed her for a hug. He held her a lot longer than she'd thought he would have in a room full of people, but she wasn't complaining. She was more than positive he still had the attention of every woman in there. Too bad he was there for Jocelynn only.

"You smell so good." He pulled away and touched her hair. "I like your hair like this. It looks good." He removed his hand from the big waves in her head and kissed her mouth before letting her go so that they could sit down. "If you weren't already pregnant, I might have to knock your ass up again looking this good." Uzoma hadn't stopped looking at her and complimenting her since he'd gotten to her.

Joc was smiling so hard she could feel her face heating up. He was always doing that, and she still didn't know how to take it. She was so used to being belittled that she sometimes thought his compliments were fake. His hand was still touching her hair, and he was still staring at her, so apparently, he really was liking what he saw. It was crazy how she felt plain but he saw more.

All she'd done was wash her hair and braid it down so that it would be wavy, and braided a quick braid across the front like she always did to use it as a headband, and throw on some jeans and a sweater with her wheat Timberland boots. Her jewelry was regular and her face was bare, but he was making her feel like she'd just stepped off the runway somewhere.

"You talking about me, but you got everybody baby mama up in here checking for you, with your sexy ass," Joc was smiling all up in his face as he draped his arm behind her chair.

The light red color that flushed across his skin turned into the cutest background for the dark brown freckles covering his face. The twinkle in his hazel eyes made Joc's heart skip a beat.

"I should kick your ass for trying to surprise me, but you're making my panties too wet right now, so I won't," Joc whispered into his ear.

When Uzoma laughed, it was as if the entire office went quiet again. Cleary, he still had everyone's attention. Joc was too busy looking at him to look at anyone else, but she could feel their eyes.

"Your fast ass. That's why we're here now." He stretched his legs out in front of him while still looking at her.

"I can't help it. You're so fucking sexy, all I can think about is sex when you're around."

Uzoma blushed again before licking his lips. "Well, keep it wet for me and I'll bust you down real quick when we leave here."

Joc squealed in excitement and clapped her hands playfully. "Oh, yes daddy!" She said a little louder than she'd intended to.

Uzoma looked around and chuckled but stopped once his eyes

135

landed in front of them. Joc didn't even have to look to know that he'd just spotted Promise. His gaze remained there for so long she had to turn around and see what Promise was doing.

Uzoma's gaze was like nothing she'd ever seen before. It made you feel like a speck of dust within seconds. He would literally make you question everything about your appearance without even saying anything. When she turned around and saw Promise staring back at Uzoma, she began to bite her tongue.

She knew Promise wasn't a punk or anything like that, but Uzoma was still more intimidating. She was actually surprised that he had the nerve to be still staring back at Uzoma.

"They said I'm getting an ultrasound today instead of a regular visit." Joc tried to break the staring match between the two of them. "So, we get to see the baby." She grabbed his hand and held it in her lap.

Uzoma kept his eyes on Promise. "That's good, baby. I can't wait."

"Uzoma," Joc called his name, but he didn't budge.

She looked from him to Promise, and they were both still shooting murderous glares at each other. Joc already knew it wouldn't take Promise too much longer to get out of pocket, and she didn't need that. Uzoma would probably kill his ass in that doctor's office, and she most definitely didn't want that.

To ease the tension, she kissed the side of his mouth a few times before running her hand across his stomach. Her lips touched the side of his mouth a few more times before she leaned further over and kissed his lips. Because she was sitting to the side of him her kisses were lopsided but once he smiled, she knew he got the point.

"When you came in here and asked for me, I almost melted. You're so fucking fine it's ridiculous." She kissed his mouth as she whispered against the side of his face. "I just be wanting to pop my pussy all over you whenever you come around." She moaned and closed her eyes as she went from kissing the side of his face to smelling along his neck. "You want to know what else I was thinking?"

He fidgeted around in his seat some before finally breaking his eye contact with Promise and turning his head to the side so that he could see her a little better. He squeezed her closer to him with the arm that was around the back of her chair.

"I was thinking about sexy you look when I be sucking you up. Your face be frowning and your eyes be rolling and shit. Then, when you put your hand on the back of my head making me go deeper…" Joc sighed into his ear. "Boyyyyyyyy." She giggled.

"Jocelynn?" He called her name in a stern voice. "You want to stay at your appointment?"

Joc looked at him with a straight face and nodded.

"Well stop talking like that." He looked at her with burning irises of fire. "You know how I get with you."

The seriousness of his voice regarding their sex life was always such a turn on for her. He played no games when it came to her and the love they made, and he made that very clear every time she tried to joke about it. If he knew how bad it made her pussy jump, he would stop because that only made her fiend for him worse.

"Why you so perfect?" Joc looked at him with googly eyes.

"I had to match you."

Her whole body warmed and she wanted to curse the little Youngblood growing in her womb for the tears forming in her eyes. She had been such a crybaby since getting pregnant. Especially when it had something to do with Uzoma. He could do or say the smallest thing and she would be in tears. He thought it was funny, but she was so embarrassed by it.

"Here we go again." He chuckled before pulling her head toward his mouth and kissing her forehead. "What's the tears for this time?"

Joc sniffed harder to no avail because her tears kept coming. "Because..." She wiped at the tears with the back of her hand.

"Because you're just so perfect to me," she told him and lay her head against his shoulder.

Uzoma laughed a little before squeezing her closer to him. "You've got to stop this shit. Got people looking at you like something is wrong with you for real."

Joc giggled as she wiped her face. "It is."

"No it ain't. I just be giving you this good dick, and now you can't control your fucking self."

Joc and Uzoma laughed together at his remark. They were laughing so hard that she'd almost missed the sounds of Promise and Risha arguing.

"Nigga, don't get mad with me because your bitch moved on."

"Shut the fuck up talking to me, B, straight up before I knock your ass out," Promise told her. "Matter of fact, hit me when you're ready. They're taking too long up in this bitch." Promise got out of his chair and passed Joc and Uzoma in a huff.

Joc wanted so badly to watch him storm out of the building because she knew he was pouting, but she didn't want to alarm Uzoma so she kept her head straight. Uzoma, on the other hand, did no such thing. He watched Promise walk out of the building before trying to stand to his feet, but Joc stopped him.

"Where you going?" She looked at him.

"I need to holla at him real quick."

"About what?" Risha's voice interrupted what Joc was about to say.

Joc and Uzoma both looked at her like the out of order bitch that she was. "Bitch, worry about your nigga, not mine," Joc told her.

"I am. Yours said he needs to holla at him, so I'm trying to see what for," Risha sassed.

"Women shouldn't get into the business of men. Mind your manners," Uzoma told her coldly before looking back at Joc. "I'll

141

be right back."

Joc pleaded with her eyes for him to stay once he stood up. She wanted to tell him to stay inside because she really didn't want any problems, but she also knew that if Uzoma wanted to do something, then he was going to do it.

"Jocelynn Waters," the nurse yelled from behind them.

Thank God.

Joc breathed a sigh of relief when she stood to grab her things.

Uzoma turned back around and looked at her with a smirk on his face. "Me and that nigga gon' have our moment."

Joc grabbed his hand and pulled him along with her. "I'm glad it ain't today."

Once they got into the ultrasound room and the nurse had Joc ready and prepped, Uzoma grabbed her hand and held it. She was over the moon excited to see her baby, and from the looks of things, so was Uzoma. He had pulled his chair closer to her bed and could almost reach out and touch the monitor where the baby would be shown.

The nurse went over the necessary information before sliding the probe over the warm gel that was on her stomach. Joc could hardly contain herself once the baby actually popped up on her screen. She was so enthralled in trying to figure out what she was seeing that she hadn't noticed anything out of the ordinary until Uzoma spoke.

"Is that two babies?" His question had Joc's head whipping around in the nurse's direction.

The nurse snickered. "Yes sir, that would be right." She circled the screen and labeled Twin A and Twin B. "Looks like they're sharing a placenta, so mom, it looks like you're going to have two of the same faces running around in a few months."

Joc was still staring at the screen. She could hear the nurse and Uzoma talking, but she was still focused on the fact that there were two babies in her stomach. Though she'd mentally accepted the fact

143

that she was about to be a mom, being a mom to two people was taking her breath away. Was she ready for that shit? Joc lay her head back and closed her eyes. What in the hell had she done?

Uzoma's hand on her head made her eyes open. "You okay?" He was now standing over her, looking down into her face.

"No." She shook her head from side to side. "I don't think I am."

Uzoma's face held concern as he looked at her. "It's going to be okay. I'ma be there to help you."

"Two babies, Uzoma?" He was too calm for her liking. "We're about to have two fucking kids."

The nurse chuckled in the background while Uzoma frowned a little.

"I can take care of all of y'all. Why you tripping?"

Joc bucked her eyes at him like he couldn't be serious right then. "You don't understand."

144

"I really don't," he told her in a tone that she didn't too much care for.

Joc sighed and sat back up so that she could see the screen. She didn't have the time for Uzoma's ole extra parental ass right then. She was stressed the fuck out, and he was acting like it was no big deal. The nurse measured both babies, checking to make sure they were both growing accurately and on time.

"These little bambinos are so long already," the nurse told them both as she measured the second twin from head to toe. "Looks like they'll fit right in with you two."

"Fit right in with me," Uzoma sneered. "Apparently, their mama doesn't want them."

Joc looked at him when she heard the tone of his voice. "Uzoma, leave me alone right now, okay? I'm in the right mood to slap your ass."

"Well, that makes two of us, so slap me if you want to and I'ma

145

slap your ass back."

Like she'd done before, the nurse snickered to herself. Joc couldn't even blame the lady, though. She could only imagine how she and Uzoma must have sounded right then.

"He's stupid." Joc waved him off. "Are they okay?" She gave the nurse her attention.

"Yes, ma'am. They're both just fine. You're measuring at thirteen weeks and five days." She was smiling when she turned the screen toward Joc and pointed. "You see this right here, that's baby A's little wee-wee. It looks like you guys are going to have a son soon."

Joc's eyes bulged. "How you know?"

"Boys tend to show a little faster than girls, so I figured I'd give you both something to lighten the mood. Hope I didn't ruin anything."

"Nah, that's what's up. You're good. Thank you." Uzoma stood up with his arms folded across his chest smiling.

The excitement in his voice could be heard loud and clear, and it almost made Joc happy.

"What's the second one?" Uzoma asked her.

She turned the screen so that it was facing him before pointing again. "Looks to me like an—"

"Another wee-wee," Joc beamed.

The nurse smiled and nodded. "Yes, ma'am. Two identical little boys."

Joc had always said she wanted all boys, and to find out she was having two babies, and they were both boys had indeed made her happy. It had taken her a second to come to terms with two kids, but seeing their little bodies growing and their father's excitement put her back in a good mood.

Uzoma was smiling hard as hell when he turned around and kissed her mouth sloppily. "They gon' be the truth, baby, watch and see." He kissed her again.

"They're going to be so cute." Joc beamed proudly. "I can't wait to see their little faces."

The nurse was busy wiping her stomach off and wrapping up her ultrasound as she and Uzoma basked in the joy of their children's sex. When they finally finished everything, she printed them both a few pictures and sent them on their way. Joc and Uzoma held hands as they exited the building, drawing stares from almost everybody in there.

Joc was no longer sure whether they were looking at her, him, or them both, but she didn't care either. She was too high in the sky to pay attention to anything that didn't concern her, Uzoma, or their boys.

Chapter 6: It hurts on the inside

Two weeks later...

"You sure that's everything?" Uzoma stood in the middle of Joc's empty apartment.

"I think so. I got rid of everything else."

"So, what your daddy say about this?" Brasi asked her.

He, Kindo, and Lu had flown to Brooklyn with Uzoma earlier that week to get Joc moved.

"He said for me not to worry about him, he's fine." Joc sniffed. "He said he may visit when the boys come." She fanned her eyes to stop her tears.

"Bruh, why you ask her about her daddy?" Uzoma walked over to where she was, grabbed her neck, and kissed her. "Y'all know she cry about anything."

Lu and Brasi both burst out laughing, but only Lu said anything. "Bitch, get your fucking life together. Ain't nobody got time for your crybaby ass for the next few months."

"Leave me alone, Lucy." Joc wiped her face again.

The five of them continued to make jokes and talk while they made sure Joc's spot was completely ready for her move out. It took pretty much the entire day for them to get everything in order before they were in the hotel rooms they'd gotten for the night.

Their flight back to Georgia didn't depart until the next day. Kindo had already begun his drive back to Georgia with all of her things, so that was one less thing they had to worry about. Uzoma had spent the past two weeks getting everything set up and ready for her so that her move would go as easy as possible, and just like he'd planned, it did.

Uzoma had just stepped out of the shower and wrapped the

towel around his waist when he saw the red light flashing on his phone. He picked it up and noticed that it was an email alert. He sighed before setting his phone back down where it had been and continued drying off.

He honestly didn't have time for Yannick's shit right then. He didn't even have to check it to know that it was her. She was practically the only person that emailed him, and she made sure to do that shit at least three times a day. Over the past week, she had even gotten a little worse.

Uzoma still hadn't figured out how in the world she'd found out about Joc being pregnant because ever since she had, she had been emailing nonstop. At least twice a day she was messaging him asking all types of crazy shit like how could he do her like that, and what did that American girl have that she didn't.

Just plain ole stupid shit that Uzoma had no interest in entertaining. He and Yannick had been over for years, and she refused to accept it. Maybe it was because he kept in such close

151

contact with her even after the breakup. That was his fault, but still hers too because he made sure to keep it strictly platonic.

Never insinuating any type of relationship that surpassed friendship, barely any phone calls, no visits, no letters, nothing more than money when she asked for it. True enough, he probably shouldn't have been doing that either, but he felt that as friends there was no reason he had to deny her.

He knew how she was living there, and his money helped. She and him had been a thing since he'd been a boy, so of course she held a special place in his heart, but that was it. The love he'd once had for her was gone. No more were the feelings of comfort and contentment. That had been placed elsewhere, and she acted like she couldn't take that.

It had been on his mind for a while to tell Joc about her, but he still felt that Joc was too timid to handle something like that. He didn't want her doubting him and the way he felt about her because of a past relationship. She was still a bit too fragile emotionally, and that would surely set the relationship he was building with her back too far.

He just felt so bad about hiding it from her. He didn't want Joc to assume there was still something for Yannick in his heart when it wasn't. He just loved her and wasn't ready to allow anything to come between them, especially not Yannick. She was old news. Joc was his life now, and he planned to show her that in every way.

"It sure is taking you a long time in here." Joc walked into the bathroom in nothing but his tank top.

"I just got out."

She eyed his wet body through the mirror. "I see." Her eyes searched his for a second before she turned and left the bathroom again.

He wasn't sure what it was, but she seemed a bit off. She had been fine before he got into the shower, but for some reason she looked a little sad or something. Uzoma briefly wondered what

153

could have bothered her that fast, but he figured it might have been the babies. Her emotions were pretty all over the place these days.

He was just about to leave the bathroom, but remembered the email from Yannick. Uzoma looked over his shoulder and noticed Joc was back lying on the bed, so he tapped on his screen quickly and pulled the phone up to his face so he could read what she'd written.

From: Yannick Njanka

[mailto:YannickNjanka@yahoo.com]

Sent: Wednesday, February 3, 2017 10:56 PM

To: Uzoma Youngblood

Uzoma, my love. Why haven't I spoken to you yet? I'm really hurting about your offspring with your American girl. You told me you loved me, why would all of this change so abruptly? Does she have your heart now? Is your heart not big enough for us both? Is there enough room there for her too? I want it all to myself. Your children are innocent, but not her. She's a thief. Only a woman with improper upbringing would chase a man who belongs to another. Does our love mean nothing to you anymore? Does her babies mean more than ours? Does the son we share not mean anything to you anymore? It was your words that promised me forever, has forever come to an end this fast? I wish to see you. Will you come? I love you, Uzoma.

Uzoma stared at the phone for a moment just staring at the message. That was the shit that got to him every time. Why couldn't she just let it go and leave things as they were? He and she were no longer together, yet she still spoke as if they were. Then to bring up their child was even worse.

What did she mean did he not love his son with her? Of course, he did. Why wouldn't he? He'd never stop just because he didn't see him every day. Uzoma took a deep breath before replying to her message.

Yannick,

I'll never stop loving our son.

He didn't even bother to address any of the other things she'd spoken on. He honestly just didn't have the time or the patience. He didn't want to hurt Yannick, but he wasn't in the mood to break her heart and wake up to fifty thousand emails either. After he closed their email, he walked out of that bathroom and into the bedroom where Joc was lying.

She was curled up into a small ball facing the wall away from him. The TV was on, but she didn't seem to be watching it, so he picked up the remote to turn it off. He then flipped the lights off and removed the towel from his waist before sliding into the soft bed behind her.

He scooted as close as he could to her and wrapped his arm around her waist. Her hair was up in a ball wrapped up with her scarf, so he was able to nuzzle her neck. She had showered before him so she smelled soft and sweet. Her soap was faint, but he could still smell it.

He inhaled deeper, and the only thing he could think while holding her was how much he wanted to be with her. How happy he was when she was around. The secure feeling in his gut when he thought of the way she felt about him. Unquestioned loyalty that she showed him daily, how sweet her smile was whenever he walked into a room. The way she submitted to his every request. The constant emptiness he felt whenever she had been in Brooklynn while he was in Georgia. All of that paired with the warm feeling that spread through him at just the thought of her had him sure about his next words.

"I love you, Jocelynn." He pressed his lips to the back of her neck. "I love you deep in my heart."

He wasn't sure if she was awake, but something about her posture and breathing let him know that more than likely she was awake. However, his mind began to wonder again when she didn't respond. Uzoma waited for a few more minutes before turning her over so the he could see her face.

Joc's eyes were red like she'd been crying, and her cheeks were moist from the fresh tears spilling down them. She tried to look away when they made eye contact, but Uzoma pulled her face back toward him.

"What's wrong, Jocelynn?" He scrunched his eyebrows up at her. "Talk to me, baby. What's the matter?"

Her tears came even harder then. She looked away again, and this time he allowed her to. Apparently, looking at him was too much at the moment. Her body rocked subtly in his arms as she tried to control the sobs that were taking over her body.

Uzoma knew the baby had her on an emotional rollercoaster, but something about her tears right then was different. They weren't hormonal tears, they were real ones. Was she happy about hearing him say I love you for the first time? Or was it the fact that she knew his love for her was genuine?

He was baffled as to what it could have been, but it was really starting to worry him. She looked like she was in some sort of pain

158

as he stared down at her. She was trying her hardest to calm herself down, but nothing was working.

"Jocelynn, baby please tell me what's wrong with you."

She shook her head from side to side and looked back at him with a face full of pain and emotion.

"I love you too… so much." She wrapped her arms around his neck and hugged him down to her.

Uzoma went willingly, wrapping his arms around her the best he could. Joc held onto him tightly until she finally let go. Once she did, she flipped back over and turned her back to him. Uzoma sat up behind her confused by her actions.

She'd just told him that she loved him, but now she was giving him her back to look at. He was confused as ever, but there wasn't anything he could do if she didn't talk to him about it. Uzoma sat still behind, her watching her shoulders move every so often due to her crying.

159

The soft continuous sniffling made his chest hurt just a tad because his baby was truly a fragile female. He watched her crying about something that was clearly bothering her, and knew for sure then that he could never tell her about Yannick. She wouldn't understand, and it would be way too much for her to handle.

There would be no easy way to tell her that his ex-girlfriend was still in love with him without hurting her, and he would never allow that to happen on his watch. There was really nothing he could do at the moment to ease whatever it was that Joc was going through, but he wanted to be near her, so he scooted back down behind her.

His hand went to her body, resting on her side until he felt compelled to touch her. He had to make her feel better, he just had to, and the only way he could do that at the moment was with sex. She refused to use words, so he would use his body. He was good at that.

Uzoma pushed the covers back, exposing both of their bodies. Without uttering any words to her, he flipped her body over softly and straddled her before pulling the thin tank top up and over her body. She was naked beneath it, so they were both nude within seconds.

She lay still, staring up at him blankly and letting him have his way with her. With expertise and precision, Uzoma eased his way down her body until he was between her legs. With her thighs on either side of his head, he was face to face with the warm entrance that not only eased his mind, but the place that would eventually welcome his boys into the world.

Just the thought of her doing something that selfless for him made him want to kiss her there. Not many women jumped at the idea of giving birth to children, but Joc was going to do it, and not to just one, but two babies for him.

Uzoma's mouth found her opening and placed kisses all over it. Her body jumped back some as he licked his lips before swirling his tongue around her folds and deep into her already leaking valley of love. Her thighs tensed up in the palms of his hands as he licked her faster, then slower, only to speed up again.

Uzoma sucked softly on the inside of each of her thighs before going back to her pussy and licking with the perfect amount of pressure for her. He'd become quite acquainted with Joc's body, and he knew that before long she would be dripping all the love he'd been craving all day onto his face.

With one hand, he pushed his hair from her face and looked up at her. She was looking down at him with flushed cheeks and a look of determination on her face. Uzoma maintained eye contact with her until her stomach tightened and she threw her head back onto the bed.

Her loud moan sounded out throughout the room as she enjoyed the feeling that his tongue had given her. Uzoma sucked a little lighter until she began scooting away and pushing his forehead. When he knew she could no longer take the feel of his mouth on her, he sat up and kneeled in front of her.

He pushed his hair back once more so that he could look at her, before grabbing the base of his dick and giving it a light squeeze. The length of him was just enough to close the distance between the two of them. His erection stretched from him to her, teasing the tip of her still dripping pussy.

Like it did every other time she was near him, it found its way to her opening and slid in without his help. Uzoma sat back on his haunches, watching her and the way her body effortlessly responded to his. Versus looking between them at their connection, she kept her eyes on him and waited for the loving he was about to give her.

Her chest rose and fell in anticipation as he tormented her with just the head. Uzoma was enjoying the view of her beautiful face and body. The light illuminated the soft, smooth skin that adorned her perfect body.

His heart beat fast in his chest as he pushed himself into her. Instantly, her legs circled his waist and tightened around him. The surge of energy in Uzoma's body shot off the map that fast. The feeling of her legs wrapped around him while observing the pleasure that had her face distorted fueled him to go deeper.

He pushed forward, feeding her every inch of him. Her mouth opened and she yelped out loud from the pain. Uzoma's face scrunched up in the pure feeling of bliss as he felt her walls contracting around him. With the hand that wasn't holding onto her waist, Uzoma grabbed the front of her neck and picked her head up from the bed.

"I love the way you feel," he grunted while looking into her eyes. "Fuck!" He groaned before falling onto her. "I love when we make love, Jocelynn."

His hand remained on her neck as he stroked her body over and over. Each thrust harder than before. Uzoma's body got hot and tingly when he heard her whimper into his ear.

"My feelings for you, Jocelynn." He pushed deep, making her gasp. "Are unconditional, baby." He kissed her ear. "I was meant for you, girl." He kissed the side of her face. "And you were meant for me." He stroked her harder and harder.

He was going so fast and hard that he was moving her whole body with just his dick. She was moaning and crying into his ear as he worked her body over with every emotion that he had for her.

"Touch me, Jocelynn," he demanded.

Her arms went around his neck, immediately forcing him to let her neck go. Uzoma gazed at her face as she stared back at his. His body was much larger than hers as he admired her frame lying beneath his. He kissed her neck, touched, and licked her breasts. He did almost any and everything he could, trying his best to prolong his orgasm.

"You love me, Jocelynn?" Uzoma asked her.

She hadn't said it back when he'd told her, not that he wanted to force her to or anything like that, but he wanted to hear it. Well, he needed to hear it. After watching Joc cry, and reading Yannick's message questioning his love for Jocelynn, he needed to hear it again. He had to make sure what he felt for her wasn't on the verge of exploding in his face.

Yannick had left him and shattered everything he'd ever thought felt good to him, and though he didn't see Jocelynn doing that, her words would assure him. Temporarily anyway.

"Jocelynn!" He yelled out when he felt her body arch up off of the bed.

She was squeezing her thick thighs around him and clawing at his back as she held her eyes closed. Uzoma watched her orgasm take over her body and lost the fight to his climax. His movements quickened until he felt the warm sensation of euphoria spread over him. Uzoma's eyes rolled to the back of his head as bit his bottom lip to keep from grunting too loud.

Joc massaged up and down his back methodically until he'd come down from his high. He was breathing hard and sweating all over her when he finally pulled away. He was just about to reach over and pull him to her so that they could go to sleep, but she hopped up too fast.

He watched her scurry from the bed and grab the towel he'd just taken off. She wrapped it around her body the best she could before going into the bathroom. Uzoma assumed she was going to clean up, but once she closed the door behind herself, he knew whatever had been bothering her was still there.

She hadn't talked before, during, or after sex, and that wasn't like her at all. Jocelynn, loved sex, and she loved sex with him even more. Normally, he spent most of their intimate moments listening to her talk to him, so for her not to have said anything this entire time assured him that his assumptions were right.

The water from the shower disturbed him that much more. Although Jocelynn always cleaned up after sex, she didn't take full showers. A hot soapy washcloth normally did the trick for them both. He tried as hard as he could to give her some space, but that only lasted for a few minutes before he was back out of the bed and heading into the bathroom.

When he got inside she was sitting on the counter looking at the floor. He looked from her to the running shower with one of his eyebrows raised.

"You taking a shower?"

"Yeah."

"Why?"

"Because we just had sex. What do you mean, why?"

Uzoma walked closer to her and leaned on the counter next to her. "Jocelynn, what's wrong with you, and I know it's something so don't say its nothing."

"It's not." She jumped from the counter and got into the shower. "I'm just fine. Just fell into some emotions real quick, but I'm good," she yelled over the shower curtain.

Uzoma wasn't sure what he wanted to make out of the way she'd worded that last statement, but if she said she was fine, then he'd accept that and go ahead. It would come out in the wash eventually. It always did with women.

***

The people walking back and forth past them with suitcases were moving at fast paces trying to make their flights while Uzoma, Joc, Lu, and Brasi stood in the middle of the floor near their gate. They had gotten to where they were supposed to be a lot faster than they'd planned, and now had a few minutes to burn.

He and Brasi had just come back from getting the girls something to eat, and as soon as he walked up, he could tell that whatever Joc had going on, she'd shared it with Lu. The way they were whispering and speaking in a hushed tone gave them both away, and if that hadn't, then the abrupt ending to their conversation once he Brasi stopped in front of them sure did.

"Damn, y'all must have been going in on our asses." Brasi handed Lu the bag of food in his hand. "Y'all stopped talking fast as hell."

169

Lu and Joc both started laughing. Uzoma, on the other hand, found nothing funny. She could sit around and talk to Lu about her problems, but when he spoke to her she acted like she couldn't fucking talk. He had given her a break last night, but she'd carried that same attitude over, and it was getting on his last damn nerve.

"Don't be trying to keep no secrets from me and my nigga." Brasi hit Uzoma's arm playfully. "Tell 'em, bruh. If they got some shit to talk, to do that shit in front of us."

Both turned their attention to Uzoma. Lu was smiling while Joc was giving him a blank look. Nothing like the way she normally looked whenever he was around.

"I'm good. Jocelynn can keep as many secrets as she wants to keep. I ain't thinking about the shit." He watched the quick flash of hurt wash over her face before she turned her head.

He'd known his nonchalant comment would hurt her feelings, she was too sensitive for it not to, but fuck it. She wanted to act crazy as fuck and not even give him a reason why, then surely, he could

170

do the same. Without even looking her way again, Uzoma walked off and took a seat near the gate.

To help time pass by, he took out his cellphone to call Demoto and let him know that they were on their way back. The phone rang a few times before Taryn answered.

"Hey, Uzoma." She sounded chipper as always.

"What's going on, girl? What you up to?" He could see Joc turn in her seat when he said something about to talking to another woman.

Yeah, it was petty as fuck, but he honestly hadn't thought about it until he'd saw her looking at him out of his peripheral. Now that he knew she assumed he was talking to another woman, he kept up his act.

"Y'all at the house?" He turned his attention back to Taryn.

"Yeah. Me and the kids are, Moto had a contract. He won't be back until tomorrow."

Uzoma stretched his legs out in front of him before rubbing the hair on his chin. "Aight, bet. My plane lands in a few. I'll slide through when I get there."

After she told him that she would be there and to let her know when he was on his way so she could make them something to eat, they ended their call. He stuck his phone back into his pocket and was about to put his headphones back on but was stopped when they were slapped out of his hand.

Uzoma looked up with a frown on his face. The only reason he relaxed a bit was because it was Lu who had hit him. She was feisty like that, so he was going to let it slide. Especially since he already knew she was about to check him on Joc's behalf.

"Lu, keep your hands off that man," Brasi said from where he was sitting.

Lu rolled her eyes in his direction before looking back at Uzoma. "What the fuck is your problem? Don't be doing her like that."

172

Uzoma exhaled. "Doing her like what?"

"Talking shit to her then talking to other bitches on the phone."

Uzoma waved Lu off dismissively. "Man, I ain't did shit to that girl."

"I'm for real, Uzoma. Don't do that shit. She's already emotional as fuck without all of your bullshit clouding her judgement too."

"Aye, if she's fucked up, it's her own fault. I ain't did nothing to her. I've been practically begging her to tell me what's up, and she acts like she can't hear, but she ain't stopped talking your ear off since we got here."

Lu rolled her eyes at him before sucking her teeth. "It's different. I'm her best friend, of course she's going to tell me stuff."

Uzoma shot Lu a look of disdain. "And I'm her man. She should tell me stuff too, but I ain't gon' make her. She can have that shit."

"Whatever, nigga. Like I said, don't fuck over my friend like that." Lu walked off with her cane.

Uzoma's eyes followed her and noticed that Joc was no longer sitting where she had been. He looked all around their gate, but didn't see her. He leaned forward trying to see the bathrooms but he still didn't see her so he stood up to get a better look.

He couldn't be sure, but he thought he saw her at the Starbucks. That only angered him because the doctor had been very clear about her not drinking coffee too early into her pregnancy. Sucking his teeth, he headed in her direction. He pushed through people as smoothly as he could, trying to get to her. When he finally got there, they'd just called her name to grab her cup.

Before she could get to it, Uzoma grabbed it and took the lid off. He smelled it while she stood in front of him with her arms folded across her chest. She was frowning and making all kind of frustrated sighs and shit, but he didn't give a fuck about her being mad.

"What's this?"

"You got your damn nose all in it, you tell me." She rolled her eyes.

"Yo, you better tell me what the fuck this is and stop playing."

Joc snatched the cup from him, spilling some of it on the floor. Both of them looked down, trying to make sure it hadn't wasted on him.

"Aye, don't get that shit on my shoes," he warned her.

"Uzoma, whatever." Joc tried to walk off, but he grabbed her arm, stopping her.

"Throw that shit away. The doctor already told you that you can't drink the shit. I don't even know why you ran your ass over here trying to get it for anyway."

"It's hot chocolate, Uzoma, now get your damn hands off me." She snatched away and switched back to their gate.

He watched her walk away and got mad all over again. Her ass was big as shit, and looking juicier than a muthafucka in the sweatpants she had on. If she wasn't so busy being stupid, he

probably could have gotten him a quickie before the plane took off,

but fuck it. If she wanted to show her ass, then he would show his

too.

Chapter 7: I'm not the same as I used to be

Could life get any more interesting? Was there anything else lurking in the shadows ready to pop out and surprise her? Lonnie sat on the corner of Zino's bed looking out of the window at him washing his car. He was so handsome and so guarded, but she was head over heels for him.

He was nothing like the men she'd dated in real life. More like the ones she'd spent countless hours reading about in books or watching on movies. For him to just walk into her life one day and turn it all around for the better was still so shocking to her. Especially since she didn't think that had been his intention.

That kind of thing didn't happen to her. That happened to other girls. Ones she'd never met. The ones that didn't live an ordinary life like hers. Girls who lived and breathed in clubs and dark alleys got men like Zino. Not the ones with respectable jobs and lifestyles.

Zino was a rough man, and one who hid many secrets, but beneath it all, he was a sweetheart who just needed love. Though he always denied it and would probably never admit it, she could tell he wanted love. That was the one thing that he was missing, and the one thing that made him normal.

Even with him calling himself crazy every other day, having nervous breakdowns, and crying uncontrollably at cemeteries, he was still just a man that needed a woman's touch. A woman like Lonnie. She would be there for him. She would watch him, nurture him, show him real love, all he had to do was let her.

They'd both been through some things, his seemingly worse than hers, but what did that matter? At the end of the day, they deserved each other, and that was all she cared about. Lonnie had made up her mind after their first sexual encounter the other night that no matter how hard he pushed, she was staying, and that was it.

She watched him wash the car for a few more minutes all

178

googly eyed before standing up and gathering her things. It was almost time for her to go to work, and she needed to be getting ready. Her clothing was sprawled out all over his room thanks to him.

It was like since he'd gotten her body once, he felt entitled to it whenever he wanted it now. They hadn't even gotten into the house good the night before, and he was ripping off her clothing. Lonnie tried to act like she didn't like it, but deep down, she loved it more than anything. It was exciting and out of the ordinary for her.

She scratched her head as she looked around for her other shoe. She'd already picked up one of them, but she didn't see the other one anywhere. Her pants, shirt, and left shoe were all cradled in her arm as she gave the room a quick scan for the right one.

When she couldn't find it, she sat everything down and kneeled down beside the bed to see if it had been pushed under there in their haste to get undressed last night. As soon as she lifted up the bed skirt she saw it, but it was on the other side of the bed.

Instead of trying to reach all the way across the bed, Lonnie pushed the boxes that had been stacked under there neatly across the floor until her shoe pushed out on the other side. She got up from the floor quickly and walked to get her shoe.

Lonnie didn't know how or why, but on the way, she lost her balance and fell onto the boxes that had come from beneath the bed.

"Ow! Shoot!" She grabbed the toe that she'd hit on the dresser.

She was still nursing her toe when she looked down and noticed that she had fallen over Zino's Polo boot. Lonnie rolled her eye before removing herself from the pile of boxes on the floor. When she was finally able to stand up she actually felt bad for a second.

She'd crushed Zino's shoeboxes horribly. The boxes were bent and one of them had even flattened out. Lonnie covered her mouth quickly before squatting down to try to fix it. She removed the lid first so that she could fix the bottom half of the box.

Upon doing this she noticed something that she hadn't before. The box wasn't filled with shoes. Lonnie was normally a smart girl, so she didn't know how she'd missed that. Hell, had some shoes been in the box she probably wouldn't have been able to smash it as easily as she had.

Where shoes should have been, there were letters and papers. Lonnie sat still for a moment trying to decide was she going to be the nosey girlfriend or was she going to fix the box and put it back beneath the bed. Of course, she chose option one.

She thumbed through the envelopes, noticing that they were all from the same person. There were only about ten envelopes, and the rest were papers that had been stapled together or sealed with a paperclip. She was trying her best to scan over the documents before Zino came inside, but apparently, she hadn't moved fast enough.

"Lonnie, what the fuck you doing?"

Lonnie's body jumped so hard she nearly knocked the box over. When she looked over her shoulder, Zino was standing there with an irritated look on his face. His hair was still pushed back and his hands were on his hips as he stared back at her, waiting for an answer.

"Why you in my shit?"

"I was looking for my shoe, but when I was about to pick it up, I tripped over your stuff and fell onto these boxes. I was trying to fix it before you came back so you wouldn't be mad, but clearly I moved too slow."

Zino looked at her like he didn't believe a word she was saying. "Those boxes weren't even out for you to fall on, so why you lying?"

Lonnie stood up from the floor and stepped closer to him. "I'm not lying, I swear that's what happened. You should know me well enough to know that if I wanted to snoop through your stuff I would have just done it."

He was quiet as he looked at her out of the side of his eye for a minute. "You better be glad you said that shit because I was about to put you out."

Lonnie frowned. "Nigga, please. If you think you're about to get my butt then think you're tossing me out and talking to me any kind of way like you do the rest of the hoes, then you got me all kinds of messed up."

Zino moved past her and sat on his bed. "Whatever, girl. Put my shit back."

"Nope!" Lonnie kneeled back down in front of the boxes. "You're an international thot I see, got people sending you sex through the mail." She flipped through the envelopes addressed from New York.

Zino leaned to snatch them from her, but she jumped back and kept the letter that was in her hand. "Nah, don't try to snatch now."

"Put that shit back, Lonnie, I'm not playing."

"Neither am I."

The two of them tugged and pulled at each other for a few more minutes until he finally let her be and kicked the whole box over before storming out of the room. Lonnie sat on the floor wondering what had she done to make him that mad. She'd thought they were just playing around, but clearly that wasn't the case.

Versus continuing to go through his things, she put away the letter and the boxes before going to look for him. When she found him, he was in the living room sitting on the floor. The game was on, but he didn't look to be playing it.

Lonnie moved slowly and padded toward him. Once she was reached him, she took a seat on the floor next to him and waited for him to say something, but he didn't. She looked at him for a while, and the only thing that made him do was take the game off pause and begin playing it.

"You're so bipolar. I thought we were having a good time, then you just flipped out."

"Because you stay getting in my business."

Lonnie was taken aback by his tone. She frowned at him and covered her chest dramatically. "Well, excuse the fuck out of me. I will be sure to mind my own business from now own."

Lonnie was past irritated when she got up from the floor. She didn't have to stay in there with him and take his attitude. She could understand that everybody had bad days, but that nigga Zino took the cake. It didn't matter what time of day it was, he was going to find a way to have an attitude at some point about something.

When she got back into his room, she gathered her things and was preparing to take a shower so he could take her to work when he walked into the room. He stood at the door with the game controller in his hand looking at her.

"Lonnie." He called her name, but she kept moving as if she hadn't heard him. "Lonnie, I know you hear me talking to your skinny ass."

Again, she ignored him and tried to walk past him to the bathroom, but he grabbed her arm. "Wait, let me explain."

Lonnie wanted to give her attitude up right then. His face was so sexy and chocolate. Then his tone had softened, and all she could think of was the way he sounded when he told her that her pussy was his, the night before during sex. It too had sounded a little softer than his normal tone.

"Those letters are personal, and I don't like to read them."

Lonnie looked at him, but didn't say anything.

"They're from some of my old family that's locked up. When I read them, I get too sad, so I put them in that box under the bed. I always think that maybe if I don't see them, then I won't think about him."

Lonnie had tried as hard as she could to act hard, but she was either too nosey or too concerned with his personal life to let their current heart to heart pass her by.

"Why don't you want to think about him? I mean, if he's your family."

Zino leaned his head to the side as if he was trying to pop his neck. "Because it's too tough. All he talks about is me linking back up with my sister and shit, and I ain't trying to do that right now."

"Why not, Zino?" Lonnie could hear the eagerness in her voice and tried to tone it down a little. "I mean, don't you miss her?"

"Hell yeah I miss her, but that shit is over. That life we lived was painful, and I ain't trying to relive it."

"How do you know that she's still living like that?"

He was quiet for a while, just looking at the floor.

"It's not like you've talked to her to find out for sure or nothing like that. She may have turned her life around and wants no parts of the painful past, just like you."

Zino shrugged. "I don't know, Lonnie. It sounds easy, but you don't know Phoenix. She was true to her soul with that shit."

"You were too though, right?"

The room was quiet as he took a seat on the bed. "Yeah, but

still." He looked away. "Man, a lot of stuff has happened since then, shit I'm too embarrassed to speak on, shit that's changed me, and I don't want to go to her like that. I'm different now than I used to be."

Lonnie sat down on the bed next to him. "If she loves you like you love her, I'm sure she won't care. I know if it was me, I would just want to see you." Lonnie touched the side of his face. "I'll call her and talk to her if you want me to."

It took him a minute before he looked at her. "I don't know, Lonnie."

"What? You think she won't talk to me?"

He shrugged.

"Well, give me her number. I bet I can make her talk to me." Lonnie nudged his shoulder playfully. "Everybody loves me, I bet you she will too."

Zino chuckled. "Don't nobody like your ass. Everybody is just too polite to tell you the truth."

"Whatever, hater. Everybody loves me, even your mean ass." She pushed his head to the side and they shared a laugh.

"I'll think about it."

Lonnie wanted to jump for joy because maybe he would take her up on her offer and actually let her talk to his sister for him. At least he hadn't just flat out said no.

"Cool. So, until you decide, tell me the embarrassing stuff that changed you." Lonnie was still being her playful self, but Zino, on the other hand, lost all emotion in his face when he looked at her.

"I don't want you to know that either."

"I'm not going to judge you, I promise."

Zino shook his head from side to side, telling her no, but she continued to push and plead until he agreed to tell her. Lonnie sat watching him and his body movements, and judging by the discomfort in his posture, she could tell it was serious.

189

For a minute, she wanted to tell him not to worry about telling her, but if he was going to tell her, she figured she'd might as well let him. They sat next to each other, quietly waiting for the other to say something. Just when she thought he wasn't going to budge, he began to talk.

"I'm not sure if I ever told you, but before I came here, I had just got done doing a quick lil' bid I'd taken once all that shit with my old family went left. Well, when I finally got released, none of my people were in Miami anymore, so I was pretty much on my own without shit to call my own.

All I had was the clothes I'd gotten locked up in, and that wasn't shit. I went back to our old house trying to check on shit, but all of that had been seized by the government, so it wasn't much there for me there either." He paused for a minute before continuing. "So, for a few days, I went from one spot to the next, just trying to find somewhere safe to lay my head, you feel me? Miami ain't like everywhere else, especially not for a nigga like me." Zino laughed, even though it didn't sound like he thought anything he was saying was very funny. "My peoples and I put in so much work, niggas would have put a hollow tip in my head without thinking about it."

"So where did you end up going?"

"Shit…" Zino stretched his legs out in front of him. "Nowhere. I ain't have nowhere to go. I was on the streets for about a week, finding food and shelter here and there."

Lonnie was confused. "So how did you end up in Georgia?"

Zino took a deep breath before allowing the stretch of silence in his room to stretch a little further. Lonnie waited patiently for him to say something else, but she wasn't going to push. He looked to be having a hard enough time saying whatever it was that was about to come next.

"Uzoma."

Lonnie nodded. "Ohhhh okay so that's how you and him met? In Miami?"

191

Zino nodded while rubbing his hands on the front of his sweats.

"I met him my last night in Miami. It was warm as hell outside and I had just got done taking a piss behind this restaurant when these niggas came out of nowhere, laughing and talking and shit. I didn't know them or no shit like that, so I just kept my head down and kept it moving, but obviously their young asses were looking for trouble." Zino cleared his throat as Lonnie watched his chest puff out some.

His posture changed into more of an aggressive one as he sat at the end of the bed looking straight ahead at the wall.

"You know how some niggas are just lame as fuck and will do anything they can to prove to themselves and the people around them that they're hard?"

Lonnie nodded. She most definitely knew a few of those kinds of people.

"Well, in the streets, there's plenty of niggas like that, mostly the young ones, though. Real OG's know how to handle business when it comes to them. But anyway, like I was saying," Zino popped his neck and stretched his legs out in front of him again, only to pull them right back in, "I was trying to get past them niggas to get back out to the main street or whatever, and two of them stepped in my way so I couldn't get by. Now, I'm a lot of shit, but a pussy ain't one. I didn't give a fuck about it being more of them than me, I was going to thump with them niggas if that's what they wanted."

"So, did they jump you?" Lonnie was eager to know what was so embarrassing about getting jumped, and Zino was taking too long to tell the story.

Zino nodded his head and chuckled a little. "Hell yeah, they beat my ass."

Him getting beat up wasn't funny to Lonnie at all, but the way he was laughing made her think it was okay to join in. However, she only laughed for a second. She stopped the moment he started back talking. She wanted to make sure she didn't miss anything.

"So, after they beat my ass, I was still talking shit or whatever,

193

so I guess that pissed them off." He looked spaced out for a minute. "Them lil niggas started doing dumb shit after that." He shook his head. "I was laying on the ground because they had fucked me up pretty bad, which is the only reason they was able to do that fuck boy shit."

"What did they do?" Lonnie spoke softly, trying to calm him down enough to tell her what happened.

"Started pissing on me and shit." He grunted a little and looked away so that he wasn't facing her. "I was moving, trying to get out the way, but the two biggest ones grabbed me and was holding me down so I couldn't move. Though I was disgusted as fuck with myself, I wasn't about to yell out like a bitch or no shit like that. Those niggas wasn't gon' break me with some fucking piss. I had been through way worse in my life, ya feel me?"

Lonnie nodded and rubbed her hand up and down his back. She could tell the conversation was starting to be too much, so she tried to sway it in a different direction.

"So where did Uzoma come from?"

"He was in the restaurant eating. He said when he came out, he heard them laughing and cursing and shit, so he stepped a little closer to see what was going on. I didn't see him, but he told me he thought that it was a woman they were messing with, so he was about to help her."

"That seems just like him too. He's so nice and sweet."

Zino nodded. "Yeah that nigga there is solid as fuck. I'll do anything for him. I don't give a fuck what it is." Zino looked over at her. "So, if you stick with me and that nigga ever needs anything, just know I'm there. No questions asked."

Lonnie nodded. She was fine with that. Uzoma had been nice to her every time they'd met. From the sounds of it, had a spot in Zino's heart forever, so if he was with it, then so was she.

"Well, when that nigga finally got down the alley, he saw them holding me down on the ground with my umm..." He cleared his throat. "My pants down or whatever." He sped past that part quickly.

Lonnie leaned over so that she could see his face. "Oh no! Why did they pull your clothes down?"

"Why you think, Lonnie?"

Lonnie's mind went everywhere after hearing that. She didn't want to jump too far out, but the only thing she could think of was... OH NO! She gasped and covered her mouth. Her eyes were wide when she looked at him with her face covered in sympathy. It was on the tip of her tongue to ask had they actually gone as far as to actually do it, but she was too nervous, and she didn't want to embarrass him.

"Oh Zino," she said quietly.

He nodded and wiped his hand over his face quickly. "Yeah, well one of them niggas had his foot on the back of my damn head while the other ones held me down for their little gay ass ring leader to try his fucking luck, but that shit didn't go down like that." His chest swelled back up a little. "It wasn't shit I was going to be able to do, but I thank God he sent Uzoma when he did." Zino shook his head. "I probably would have killed myself for real had that shit gone down."

"Well, I thank God he came too. My life would have been so bland had I never met you." Lonnie lay her head on his shoulder and wrapped both of her arms around his. "You're so special to me."

The room was quiet as Zino sat and listened to her. He placed his hand on her thigh and squeezed it. "You're special to me too."

"If I'm real special, you'll let me call your sister."

Zino chuckled some. "You're so damn nosey."

"So? You already knew that."

"Well, like I said, I'll think about it."

"You're no fun." Lonnie got up and was about to leave the room to take a shower. "I'ma have to find me a man that's less complicated," she yelled over her shoulder.

Before she could even reach the bathroom, he was right up on her with his arms around her waist. He bit her face playfully while tickling her stomach.

"You said you're going to do what?"

"Find me another man," she managed to get out through giggles.

"Try me and see what I do. You gon' be mine forever. I dun told you all my business and shit. Your ass ain't going nowhere." He kissed her face. "You staying with me, and you better not ever try to leave."

Lonnie's heart fluttered when she heard him say that. She knew how she felt about him, but she hadn't really been sure about how he felt about her. To hear him say she'd better not ever leave made her want to stay forever. Lonnie leaving Zino was the last thing he had to worry about.

She spun around in his arms and wrapped her arms around his

neck. "How you know I want to be stuck with you forever?"

"You might as well stop your shit girl, you know you love my ass. You ain't going nowhere anyway."

Lonnie had to admit that he was right. She had absolutely no plans to go anywhere. All she wanted to do was stay and love him past his pain, starting right then. With no more talking exchanged between the two of them, Lonnie began to undress and pulled at his clothes.

She got completely naked in front of him before clawing at his clothes. Zino helped her remove his clothes before climbing into the running shower with her. They both showered before indulging in another round of shower sex, and let Lonnie tell it, it was just as good as their first encounter had been.

Zino had beat her body down so bad she could hardly feel her legs when she got out. She wasso weak, she slipped on the rug and almost fallen but Zino caught her. He laughed at how clumsy she was until she'd told him why she could barely stand.

199

He really went in on her then. He continued to make fun of her

until she'd gotten completely dressed and they were on their way to

take her to work. Though she'd been with him all day and night,

Lonnie still wasn't ready for him to go when he pulled up to the

front of her job.

"What you sitting over there looking crazy for?"

Lonnie's arms were crossed over her chest. "I don't want to go

in there."

"Girl, you better take your ass to work."

"You make me sick." Lonnie rolled her eyes and opened the

door to get out.

"Yeah... yeah... yeah... I love you too."

Lonnie paused for a minute, and looked back at him over her

shoulder. "I knew I shouldn't have gave you this ass. Look at you

thinking you're in love with me already."

Zino's handsome face lit up from his laughter, making Lonnie smile too. She was blushing super hard after hearing him tell her he loved her. She wasn't sure if he was serious or not, but she'd take that little bit for now.

"Man, get your ass out of this car."

"Nah, baby, tell me you love me again, and this time make it sound a little sweeter. Then I'll get out."

Zino reached over and pushed some of her hair out of her face before leaning over and pecking her on the lips.

"I love you… I think."

With rolling eyes, Lonnie shook her head, got out of the car and closed the door. Zino rolled the window down so she could talk to him.

"I love you too, I think."

After he winked, Lonnie walked away and headed inside to her job. She needed to get her day on a roll. She had been kicking it with Zino so much lately that it felt like that was all she was supposed to do. Whenever she was at work she was counting down the minutes for him to come back.

Once she finally made it to her desk, she put her things away before pulling out the letter that she'd taken from his house. In a small way, she felt like she was invading his privacy, but then again, she didn't. She'd learned since being with Zino that he was the kind of person who you had to make face problems, and she was going to make sure he faced them all before furthering their relationship.

She made sure to print out all of her incoming patient charts for the day before pulling the letter completely from the envelope and reading it.

Zino,

What's going on? I miss you, young blood. They got me up here at Riker's Island and this shit ain't no hoe. Niggas stay on some grimey shit, but you know me. That shit ain't fazing me at all, I'm ready to break down any one of these young niggas that try me. But anyway, I spoke to Phoenix the other day, she told me she still hasn't heard from you. Why is that? I thought I told you to hit her up? Y'all are family, Zino, y'all need each other. You two are all that's left of us, don't let the Zoo Crew die like that, man.

Tone and Tek would be fucked all the way up if they knew you and Fe didn't have each other's backs the way we raised y'all. I know you're probably still mad about the decision I made, but you have to understand, young nigga, that I've lived. I've done shit all my life, you and Fe were just beginning. I didn't want this life for y'all. I didn't call y'all my lil brother and sister for nothing. I love her, and I love your hardheaded ass. Link up with your twin, man, and get your life back on track.

Hell, link up with her ass, and both of y'all come see your big bro. Love you, young nigga, and keep your head up. I may not be there physically, but I'm always here if you need me. I know you been through some shit in life, and I don't want you to ever think you don't have anybody, I'M GONE ALWAYS BE YOUR FAMILY. ME AND FE. Don't live like you're alone, Zino. We got you. Hit me up.

Oh, and here's Fe's number again just in case you lost it in the last few letters I sent you since your ass never writes back.

Phoenix 757- 334-0097

Lonnie read the letter over a few times before diverting her eyes over to the clock on her desk. She had fifteen minutes before her shift actually started, so she hurried to the breakroom. Once she was outside, she dialed the number at the bottom of the paper. Her heart was beating fast as the phone rang, but it was now or never, and even with her being as nervous as she was, she'd rather it be now.

"Hello," a female voice came over the line.

"Umm, hey… is this Phoenix?"

The line was quiet for a moment, both of them saying nothing.

"Who is this?"

"This is Lonnie, you don't know me, but I'm your brother's

girlfriend. Well, not really, but almost. We're something like that," Lonnie rambled nervously.

"My brother? My brother who?" Fear and skepticism were all through Phoenix's words, and it kind of made Lonnie feel bad.

"Zino."

"Oh my God! Where is he?"

"He's here in Georgia. He doesn't know that I'm calling you, but he really needs you, Phoenix."

Soft sniffles could be heard through the receiver as Lonnie waited for her to speak.

"I need him too," she whimpered.

Lonnie's heart broke for them both. This was seriously something much more complicated than she'd anticipated it being, but who was better for the job than her? All she hoped was that Zino didn't kill her for what she was about to do.

Chapter 8: I'll love you enough for both of us

The little red and navy blue onesies with the basketball and baseballs all over them had to be the cutest things Joc had ever seen. They were so small, and would be perfect for the twins. Pretty much everything that she'd seen had been perfect for them in her opinion, but she couldn't get everything, so she was doing her best to narrow down her choices.

"Girl, how long are you gon' stand there with them outfits? Just get it all. Their daddy can afford it." Taryn snatched the clothes from her hand and tossed them into the cart behind them.

Joc smiled and turned to look at all the stuff she and Taryn had racked up for their boys. They had been in Target for almost an hour, stuck in the baby section. It had been almost three days since they'd been back in Columbus, and she and Taryn had been out shopping

206

every day since then.

They'd started with furniture and pictures for Joc and Uzoma's spot, but now that they'd gotten that out of the way, they were free to shop for their kids. Though shopping had never really been Joc's thing, clearly it was Taryn's. She could go from one store to the next without getting tired.

Joc, on the other hand, was good for maybe one or two stores before she was done for the day. She could already tell that hanging with Taryn was most definitely going to get her out of that.

"I just don't want to go crazy. They'd have everything up in here if I do."

"Well shit, go crazy. Uzoma can afford that shit."

Joc rolled her eyes before throwing two of the same color blankets into the basket.

"Chile, what the hell is wrong with y'all? You been walking around with that little attitude since y'all got back, and his ass ain't no better. Y'all about to get on my nerves. Y'all stay mad too much."

Taryn leaned on the cart and waited for Joc to say something.

Joc looked everywhere but at her because she hadn't realized that Taryn had noticed. True enough, she was still mad and had been since her last night in Brooklynn. It was indeed her own fault that she was mad, but it was halfway Uzoma's too. She wasn't about to dismiss her feelings just because she was nosey.

"Don't think about it, tell me." Taryn pushed further. "You're about to be down here with me, so you'd might as well make me your new best friend." She was smiling when Joc looked at her.

"You're so pretty," Joc told her.

"Girl, I know. Demoto tells me every day."

The store attendant smiled at them both as he walked past while they were laughing.

"That's so sweet. Y'all really are the cutest couple I've ever seen. I thought my friend Breon and her man, Wren, was cute, but I think you and Demoto take the cake."

Taryn flipped her long hair over her shoulder. "Well, I thought so too until you and Uzoma came along. If y'all could stop being mad all the time, y'all would definitely have us beat."

Joc looked down and shook her head. The large chunky gold earrings in her ear clinked against her neck as she moved. Some of her hair fell over her shoulder as she stared at the wheat colored Timberland boots on her feet. They were by far her favorite pair of shoes.

"I thought we were good too, you know? He came along and made me see men in a totally different light, but girl, Uzoma has two heads or something. He's all sweet to me, but still talking to his ex-girlfriend back in Cameroon."

Taryn gasped with wide eyes. "How you know?"

Joc was skeptical about telling her because although Taryn was sweet, she didn't know if she could trust her not to tell Demoto and get it back to Uzoma. Clearly, Taryn could read her mind because she spoke up before Joc was able to voice her concerns.

"And don't worry about me telling Demoto nothing. Whatever you tell me will be between me and you, I promise. I'm not even like that."

Joc looked at her smiling for a minute before shaking her head again. "Nah, girl, you're going to think I'm crazy."

Taryn sucked her teeth and waved Joc off dismissively. "Joc, please. I'm sure I've done some crazier shit than whatever it is you're about to tell me. Trust me." She giggled. "I don't play when it comes to Demoto."

Joc nodded before she began pushing her cart, with Taryn following her with hers. "Well, I hacked into his email account one night, and I've been reading the emails ever since. I hooked his email account up to mine, so when he gets a new one, it comes to my phone too."

Taryn giggled to herself before nudging Joc's arm. "I knew we were sisters or something."

Joc smiled and felt better about telling her, now that she knew Taryn could relate to her. "So, any time the girl Yannick emails him I be reading that shit, and girl why she emailed him the night before we left for Brooklynn asking him why does he love me and shit like that. Then asked him did he love our twins more than he loved the baby they got." Joc looked at Taryn with a hurt expression on her face. "Taryn-Lee, I didn't even know he already had a baby, and I can't say nothing to the nigga without him thinking I'm crazy for going through his shit."

Taryn nodded in agreement before her face frowned and she began shaking her head from side to side instead.

"Hell nah, Joc, yes the fuck you can, and you better. If he gets mad about you going through his shit, then flip it around and tell him he shouldn't have had anything in there for you to find in the first place."

Joc sighed dejectedly. "I thought about it, but Uzoma is just so sweet, and the best man I've ever had. I don't want to run him off by being crazy. He's always telling me he's not my old nigga so don't treat him like him and stuff. If he finds out I've been on some sneaky shit, he might run for the damn hills."

"No, he won't, trust me. Men try to act like they don't, but they like crazy women. To be honest, I don't think it's crazy at all. When you're dealing with someone new, it's almost like second nature to go through their shit." Taryn flipped her hair back again. "Girl, you've got to know what you're dealing with."

"So, you think I should tell him?"

Taryn nodded. "Yep." She looked around them before whispering lower. "Don't tell him I told you, but how do you think he found out you were pregnant?"

Joc frowned in confusion because she honestly hadn't thought about it.

"He had somebody watching your ass up there." Taryn snickered until Joc too started to laugh. "Girl, he was spying on you. He told me it was to keep you safe, and part of me believes that because those Youngbloods are crazy about their women, but the other part of me knows that nigga was just trying to make sure you wasn't sleeping around."

That was seriously some news to Joc. She hadn't given how he'd known she was pregnant any thought, and now that Taryn had told her, it all made sense.

"I'm glad I wasn't doing shit."

"You'd better be." Taryn stopped at the back of the checkout line. "So, you gon' tell him? I personally think you should. I guarantee you it won't be as bad as you're thinking. Uzoma is a sweetheart for real. Sweeter than Demoto, he's still going to love you."

"He really is," Joc swooned as she thought about him.

"I'm telling you, get your man before Yannick does." Taryn laughed again. "Don't let that lil African hoe and her baby steal your man."

"Okay, I'ma tell him when I get home."

Taryn shook her head from side to side. "Nah, no you won't. You're about to tell him now." Taryn nodded her head toward the door.

Uzoma and Demoto were walking in and looking like heaven on earth. They were the two most beautiful things in the store, and commanding every ounce of attention that could be given. Joc could see almost everybody at the front of the store watching them with no shame as they walked in.

They'd both worn their hair all down today, and were dressed similar in all black with mean mugs on their faces. Demoto's green eyes, and Uzoma's hazel ones were flickering with discontent as they took in their surroundings. Their entire appearance was exactly alike except the fact that Uzoma's skin was a little lighter than

214

Demoto's. Other than that, everything was the same, even the way they walked.

In Joc's opinion, they looked like two lions on the prowl for their prey. They had this predator type aura about themselves. The long steady strides they took while glowering at people with those intimidating eyes was just too much for an ordinary person.

If Joc didn't know any better, she would think they were mad, on their way to wreak havoc on some unfortunate soul. Luckily, she had become quite familiar with this. It hadn't been too long ago that Uzoma's presence alone made her feel like the smallest person in the room, and that was saying a lot since she was a relatively big woman.

"Girllllll," Joc sighed.

"I knowwwwww," Taryn chimed in, sounding just as infatuated as she did.

"I don't know if I'll ever get used to that boy."

Taryn's head shook. "You won't. I haven't." She leaned her head to the side. "Don't it make you feel good that a man who looks like that wants you?"

"Does it?' Joc agreed. She thought she was the only one who felt like that.

"I used to feel privileged to be with that nigga until I realized I was just as fine as his ass." Taryn and Joc both burst out laughing at Taryn's comment.

It was like the moment they began laughing, their resolute and unapproachable Lions became aware of their presence. Both of their heads whipped around in their direction with unwavering gazes. Eyes steadying on the things that mattered to them most. Demoto and Uzoma's eyes held the same twinkle upon spotting the women.

"Girl, you see these all these bitches hating?" Taryn whispered making Joc look around. They definitely had an audience. "You better stop being crazy and get your man. You're just as fine as he is, remember that shit. Fuck a damn Yannick. Did you see the way his face softened when he saw you just now?" Taryn's voice trailed off the closer the men got.

Though Joc didn't have time to respond to her due to them approaching a lot faster than they'd been initially walking, she'd heard her loud and clear. Lu had told her the same thing, and she was going to take their advice. They were both in happy relationships with men who worshipped the grounds they walked on, what reason did she have not to take their advice? Clearly, they knew what they were talking about.

Uzoma walked directly to her and invaded her personal space. He was so close to her that his chest was pressed against her shoulder as he ran his hand through her hair, grazing her scalp before sliding it down to her neck and pulling her head to his lips.

After a quick peck to her forehead, he leaned down some so that he could see her face. With his hand still holding on to the back of her neck, he pulled her head back some so that she was looking up at him. The glare that took her nerve every time she saw him was in place as he observed her facial expression.

"You okay?"

She nodded, lost in his eyes.

"I would ask did you have fun shopping, but I can see for myself that you did." He smiled when he looked from her to the red cart full of baby essentials.

Joc couldn't hide her smile after that. "I couldn't help myself. Everything was so cute."

Uzoma kissed her smiling lips before touching her stomach with his other hand. "I couldn't help myself either, you was just so cute." He mimicked her as he continued playfully kissing all over her face. "You still mad at me?"

Joc stopped smiling and looked at him for a minute before answering. "Yeah, but we'll talk about it when we get home. Right now, I just want to enjoy you being next to me." She kissed his chin. "With your sexy ass." Her smile spread across her face when his cheeks flushed red.

His blushing would never get old.

"I don't know why you're always blushing. You've got to know how fine you are."

"I think the same thing about you. It's crazy to me that you don't know how intriguingly beautiful you are." He stepped back and looked her up and down playfully. "It's cool though, I don't mind showing you."

"Why you don't mind?" Joc wrapped her arms around his waist, pulling his body closer to hers.

He whispered into her ear. "Because you got a fat ass and you give me good pussy."

Joc squealed in embarrassment as he squeezed her butt in both of his hands. She giggled uncontrollably into his chest as he hugged her to him.

"Man, come on girl and ring this shit up, with your silly ass."

He pushed her toward the register.

"I thought maybe y'all had forgot y'all was in the middle of Target where people and their kids are shopping with all that touching and stuff y'all was over there doing." Taryn's nose was turned up as she smirked at Joc and Uzoma.

She was leaning on her cart while Demoto stood behind her with his arm thrown loosely over her shoulder. Joc gave them a humiliated smile before putting all the things she'd picked up onto the register.

"I'm telling you. Just inappropriate as fuck." Demoto joined in with her.

Uzoma and Joc were both laughing as Taryn and Demoto stood to their side making jokes about them. When they'd finished paying for their things, they all left the store and headed back to Joc and Uzoma's apartment. Taryn had driven over there, so once they got there, she and Demoto hopped in and left, headed on their way.

Ever since Joc had told Uzoma she would tell him about why she'd been mad, her stomach had been doing flips. She was so scared to be alone with him because she knew he was going to ask her again, and she was no longer sure she had the courage to confront him anymore.

It always seemed easy in the presence of Lu or Taryn, but whenever she got alone, her mind changed immediately. She was standing in the bathroom braiding her hair down into two French braids when he appeared in the doorway in nothing but his sweatpants.

He had shed his jacket and shirt, and was looking like hot, wild, dirty sex. The long blonde locs that had been resting along his shoulders earlier were now pulled back into a ponytail at the back of his neck with a few resting along his collar bone and chest.

Both of his hands were tucked into his pockets as he stared at her through the mirror. His eyes were unmoving as he watched her braiding her hair like it was the most interesting thing he'd ever seen.

Joc stood quietly trying to milk as much time as she had before he brought their first real fight up.

"I'm waiting on you to talk to me, Jocelynn."

Fuck!

Joc wanted to roll her eyes, but since he was still looking at her, that wasn't an option. Instead, she looked over at him quickly before looking back at herself.

"I'm not going anywhere, so it really ain't no point in stalling."

"I'm not stalling," she lied.

"Well, tell me what's on your mind."

Joc pushed both of her braids over her shoulder before turning around to face him. Arguing and exposing her nosey findings was the last thing she wanted to do. The pants he was wearing did absolutely nothing to hide the large print resting along his leg.

How was she supposed to concentrate with that thing right in

222

her face like that? No woman in her right mind, let alone one who had actually had the pleasure of feeling it would be able to focus on anything else with him pushing it all into her face like he was. Joc poked her bottom lip out, pouting momentarily before she began to bite it as she thought about interrupting their moment with sex instead of talking.

"Tell me what's good, and I'll give it to you in a minute." His deep voice made the water in her panties pool even more. "You can do whatever the fuck you want to do with it after you tell me what's been bothering you."

Joc thought she was going to go crazy when he covered his dick with one hand and reached for her with the other.

"Your lil hot ass."

"Your lil hot ass. You know how I am," she told him as he led her from the bathroom and back into their bedroom.

Uzoma sat her down on the bed before taking a seat in front of her on the floor. He raised his knees up so that he could rest his arms across them comfortably before raising his eyebrows at her.

Joc sighed deeply before licking her lips and looking toward the door. As hard as she was trying, she couldn't make herself look at him while she told on herself. She just didn't have the heart for that right then.

"Jocelynn." Her name sounded more like a command than anything.

"You told me you and Yannick were over, right?" She forced herself to look at him.

"I did."

"Well, if you all are over, why does she keep emailing you like y'all are still an item?"

"I don't know."

Though his responses were short, he didn't sound rude, which was the only thing that prompted Joc to keep going. Had he sounded even the slightest bit annoyed, she probably would have lost her nerve. Uzoma was always a serious person, so she wasn't surprised at his curtness while answering her questions.

"Well, maybe if you didn't continue to reply to her, then she would stop. In my opinion, you're leading her on, unless you're actually still interested in the things she has to say."

Joc stared at Uzoma, waiting for him to say something. His face wasn't as hard as it had been moments prior, but he was still straight faced. She could tell he was thinking.

"So, you don't think I should talk to her at all?"

The fuck? Joc thought.

"No. Why should you? What do you and her have to talk about? All she does is beg and plead for your love, and you fall right into it. Giving out money, checking on her family and stuff. That is stuff a boyfriend would do, Uzoma, and unless you're her boyfriend and I just don't know it, that shit is out of line." Joc could feel herself

225

getting into combat mode.

Whenever she and Promise would argue, she would always end up in his face, yelling and putting her hands on him. She was hoping like hell that Uzoma wouldn't bring that out of her. It was just hard to control herself once she got hype, and if he didn't say the right thing soon, she could feel herself getting out of hand.

"Jocelynn, why should I be nasty to her just because we aren't together anymore? That's not the kind of man I am. Should I send her money and check on her family? Probably not, but I felt like she and I were friends, and as her friend, when she was in a bind I helped her out. I didn't see it as anything more."

"So, it's okay for me to take money from Promise and tell him how much I love him and all kinds of bullshit like that?"

Uzoma's nostrils flared as his eyes darkened. He fidgeted some on the floor before clasping his hands together.

"Hell no. You should never have to ask another nigga for shit while you're with me. That's what I'm here for. I don't care if its money, attention, sex, any fucking thing you need, I'm the only man you should address about it."

"Well, what's the difference then? You out here doing the same shit for your ex bitch that you're doing for me. I clearly don't mean very much to you." Joc hopped up from the bed and paced the floor.

"Sit down, Jocelynn."

"No! If you want the same hoe that dirted your ass just because she knew she could, then leave me alone. I don't have time to play these same games with you that I played with Promise." Joc could feel herself getting emotional. "I'm not about to do this again, Uzoma. It takes too much out of me. If you want her then please just leave me alone. Just let me go on about my business. You can still see the boys, be a good daddy, do what you have to do, but if you think I'ma sit here and play house with the same bitch that broke your heart, then you're so wrong. We don't have to be together."

Uzoma hopped from the floor and snatched her to him by her

227

arm. He pulled her to him so that he was directly in her face.

"Don't you ever tell me that we won't be together." He huffed as his eyes grew even darker. "As long as I'm breathing, you'll be mine, and you ain't got no choice about the shit either. You think when I said I love you the other night it was a joke? Because it wasn't. I love you, Jocelynn." He grabbed her other arm in his hand. "Don't talk about leaving me." He sighed. "Especially when you didn't leave that nigga Promise." He pushed her away from him some. "You didn't leave him, why would you leave me?" He was looking at her like he really didn't understand her. "I'm not the best man in the world, but I try to be for you. I spend all of my time thinking of ways to make you happy, but you're ready to leave me about some fucking emails?" He shook his head from side to side. "Nah... hell nah, that ain't happening."

"Well what do you want me to do Uzoma? It's obvious you still love the damn girl, or else you wouldn't still be talking to her." Joc's eyes watered against her will. "I can't compete with her." Joc hadn't wanted to cry, but after thinking of the pictures that Yannick had sent him in one of her emails of she and Uzoma, she couldn't hold it in.

Not only was Yannick extremely beautiful, but she and Uzoma actually looked good together. Much better than Joc felt him and her did. She'd cried her eyes out in the shower the night before after seeing the pictures. Uzoma was kissing her face on one of the pictures while she sat on his lap, and looking serious on the other one.

"What you mean you can't compete with her?" He frowned.

"I saw the pictures she sent you, Uzoma." Joc looked away from his angry face. "She's gorgeous, I see why you love her. Y'all look good together."

Where in the bloody hell his next reaction came from Joc still didn't know, but it scared the living daylights out of her. In one swift movement, Uzoma punched the wall near the door, placing a hole in it. Joc stood by as he hit it again and again, leaving a hole in the wall every time.

She wasn't sure what to do, so she just stepped back and allowed him time to release his anger. When he finally turned in her direction and walked toward her, she jumped and bumped into the dresser. She didn't think he was going to hit her or anything like that, he'd just taken her nerve for a minute.

He had gotten to her so fast and he was still looking very angry. Uzoma totally disregarded her fear and grabbed her by both of her arms before shaking her lightly.

"What the fuck is wrong with you, Jocelynn? You're the most beautiful woman on the fucking planet. Why won't you just see that shit? I don't give a fuck about Yannick being gorgeous. That shit doesn't mean anything to me because I love you. I see you with more than my eyes, Jocelynn." He exhaled in exhaustion. "I see you with my heart, baby, and that's all that matters to me. I want to love you, I want to keep you, I want you to feel the same way about me that I feel about you, but clearly you don't know how."

Joc looked away from him and he turned her face back toward him.

"No, look at me when I'm talking to you." He held the bottom of her face so that she had to look at him.

His beautifully angry face.

"If you can't love yourself right now, Jocelynn, I'll do it until you can. I'll love you enough for both of us, but you have to let me. Stop saying that weak bitch shit about you not being able to compete with her. Fuck all of that. You're sexy as hell, and you need to recognize that shit. There ain't shit that Yannick can offer me that I'd want again. Just like you said, she dirted me, so that shit is over. I don't care if I send her a million emails, which I won't anymore since now I know it bothers you, that shit don't mean nothing. She can never have me again, Jocelynn. Ever. You hear me?"

Joc tried to wipe her face to keep the tears from coming but he was still holding onto both of her arms and she couldn't really move them.

231

"I asked did you hear me. Open your mouth and talk. You had a mouth full to say a minute ago." Uzoma was forceful with her.

"I hear you," she said through her tears.

"Well, make this the last time you compare yourself to her. Who gives a fuck how good we used to look together, you and I look better." Uzoma finally let her go and went to grab his phone.

He snatched her right back to him once he had it in his hand and tapped the screen. As soon as it lit up, a picture of her and him popped up. She was laughing and looking off to the side, but he was looking at her. His face was serious and looked to be deeply enthralled by her.

Joc didn't know when the picture had been taken, nor had she ever seen it, but it was breathtaking. She looked so bubbly while his focus was solely on her. The gaze she was accustomed to feeling, felt even more powerful in that picture.

"You see how good we look together?"

Joc nodded.

"You didn't even know I took the picture. You were too busy being happy about being back with me. I took this in Brooklynn at the mall that day."

Joc still didn't remember, but she didn't bother to say that.

"Can you tell how enamored I am with you, Jocelynn? I didn't even notice how deep I'd fallen for you until I looked back at this picture. It's all over my damn face. I want you to feel the same way about me, Jocelynn."

"I do."

"No, you don't, because if you did, you wouldn't be intimidated by a fucking email because you would already know ain't nobody fucking with my heart when it comes to you."

Joc could literally feel her legs weakening as she listened to him talk. He was so unnerving. How could one man be so perfect? After listening and watching the way he exemplified his love for her, Joc felt crazy for allowing herself to fall into her feelings that deeply.

"What about the baby, Uzoma? The one you have with her?"

It was then that Joc began to doubt herself again. The look that washed across his face was one that scared her. The anguish and emotion that he rarely showed had returned. He held his head down and took a deep breath.

"What about him?"

"Why didn't you tell me about him? You don't think I should have known that you have a son?"

Uzoma let her go and sat down on the bed. "Had..." He looked up at her. "I had a son. She had an abortion when she was seven months."

All the wind in Joc's body almost left her upon hearing that. Why in the hell would she do that? Most importantly why would she wait so long to do it?

"That little bitch. Why she talk about him like he's still here then?" Joc got mad at Yannick that fast for being such a fuck up.

He shrugged. "I don't know, Jocelynn. I've asked her to stop even bringing him up, but she won't."

"She's so stupid."

Uzoma nodded but didn't say anything else. It was clear he had been and still was very fucked up over their son. Joc could understand, though. She hadn't even known she was pregnant for very long, but she felt an attachment to the twins that she couldn't even explain. There was no way she could do something like that to them.

"Listen, Jocelynn, I love you baby for real. I know you're used to being lied to and cheated on, but that's not me. I'm not going to do you like that, okay? Just trust me. You have no reason to be around here playing Inspector Gadget, aight?"

Joc fell onto his shoulder laughing. "I love you too."

Uzoma turned to the side, making her head fall from his

shoulder. He scooted back some before removing his sweatpants while Joc looked on in confusion.

"Boy, what are you doing?"

"I want to hear you say that while you're riding my dick." He lay back on the bed and pulled her on top of him. "It's got to sound better when you're moaning."

Joc's body got hot as she began to remove her clothing. Once she was naked, she kissed every spot of him that she could see before connecting them in the way that they'd both been yearning for all day. In her mind, Uzoma telling her that he loved her was the best thing she'd ever heard, but she had to admit, it sounded much better when he moaned it as well.

Chapter 9: Oh my god! That's my baby

"Nigga, I told your punk ass you was in love." Uzoma chuckled as he listened to Zino talk to him about Lonnie.

"I ain't gon' say all of that, but she does have a nigga kind of open."

"Bruh, I don't know why you fighting the shit. Get the girl and let her change you. Ain't nothing wrong with having a good woman. Love ain't all bad, Zino."

Though Zino didn't talk much about it, Uzoma knew enough about him to know that he was afraid to love and be loved. Uzoma couldn't blame him, though. After Zino told him about his past, he couldn't really blame him for being the way he was.

"I hear you, I'm thinking about it. How's you and Jocelynn?"

Uzoma smiled at just the mention of her name. "In love as shit."

They shared a laugh. "But nah, for real, happy as hell. I'm out now about to get her some flowers and shit. She been sick as hell with them babies."

"Check your ole cake daddy ass out."

"Ain't nothing wrong with being a cake for your girl, nigga. You need to take notes,"

Zino was laughing. "I'm taking notes, nigga. I'm about to go grab this loud mouth ass girl some flowers right now too then."

Uzoma chuckled as he pointed at the large bouquet of red roses for the lady to grab. "That's right, lil nigga, make me proud."

The two of them spent a little more time on the phone tripping out before Zino told him that he would call him back later because Lonnie was about to get in the car. Once Uzoma hung up the phone, he paid for Joc's roses before leaving the flower shop.

It was Friday evening and she had been sick all week. He'd

238

wanted to take her out on a date or something just to get her out of the house, but from the way she sounded when he'd talked to her on the phone earlier, that probably wasn't going to happen.

Uzoma rode down the street listening to his music, thinking about something he could do for her at home that would make her just as happy, but he couldn't think of anything. Maybe once he got there she would change her mind about them going out.

When he finally pulled up to their spot and went in, she was lying down on the sofa staring at her phone. He didn't even have to ask to know that she was reading. That was all she did. He almost thought she read a little more now since finding out that reading while pregnant supposedly made your baby smarter. She had been a damn Kindle addict since then.

"What's going on, beautiful? How you feeling?"

She looked up at him and smiled. "Better, you look so cute. Where you been?"

Uzoma had just left the Natural hair shop getting his hair re-twisted and styled, so he was sure that's what she was referring to.

"Out trying to get sexy for this lil chick I've been checking for but she keeps playing a nigga to the left,"

Joc frowned. "You mean to tell me there's a bitch out there turning down somebody as fine as you?" Joc shook her head. "Something is wrong with that hoe. You don't need her, it's clear she doesn't care about life."

"Nah, I ain't gon' say all of that. Shawty just pregnant, so she don't really be feeling that good." He walked all the way in and closed the door behind him.

"So, she's pregnant and stupid? Nah, you don't need her."

Uzoma smiled as he took a seat on the sofa next to her. "Well, what do I need then?"

Joc pushed the covers from her body and straddled his lap. "Me."

240

He smiled as he took her lips with his own. They engaged in a passionate kiss that lasted way longer than it probably should have before pulling apart. Joc was still smiling at him, as he was her.

"You feel like getting out?"

Joc leaned her head to the side before nodding. "Yeah, we can do something."

"Well, let's get dressed."

It took Uzoma a little over thirty minutes to get ready while Joc was still in the bathroom doing her hair. When he walked to the door to see if she was ready, his heart began to beat fast. She was braiding her signature braid across the front of her head and looking so pretty.

His sons had her glowing like an angel. Her face was a little chunkier, but it looked like it had an extra light shining on it or something. His eyes trailed from her head to her stomach. She was in nothing but her bra and jeans, giving him time to admire the round bulge that her stomach had formed into.

241

She wasn't too huge yet, but it was definitely noticeable. He checked her stomach out for a few moments longer before allowing his eyes the pleasure of her widening backside. Since she'd been carrying the twins, her ass had gotten so much larger than it was before, which worked in his favor.

Jocelynn complained about her weight gain every day, but Uzoma was loving it. He had always been a man who appreciated a heavier woman, and though Jocelynn was far from it, the extra pounds made his dick hard.

"Why you staring at me, Uzoma Youngblood?"

"Because I'm in love like hell, girl. You got me standing back here feeling like a bitch with my stomach and heart fluttering and shit."

Jocelynn held her head down as she tried to hide her smile. Anytime he complimented her she would get bashful. It was cute to him, so he made sure to do it regularly. Not to mention, he never wanted her to feel less than she was. It was his job to keep her head in the clouds, and he had not one issue with it.

"I'm getting fat."

Uzoma walked up behind her and rested his chin on her shoulder as she spread lip gloss over her lips. "You're carrying two babies, Jocelynn, you're going to gain some weight." He gripped her thighs in his hands. "I don't know why you tripping anyway, I love this shit. I hope you keep every pound, even after the boys get here."

Uzoma couldn't stop the laugh that escaped his mouth when she looked at him. She looked mortified.

"Why would you say that? Oh, my goodness. God forbid," she expressed herself dramatically.

Uzoma didn't even bother to acknowledge her silliness. Instead, he kissed the side of her face, smacked her butt, and told her to hurry up. She quickened her pace and was ready within the next few minutes. Uzoma pulled his car into the parking lot at the restaurant and parked before going to her side to help her out. He grabbed her hand before moving to cross the street.

Demoto had told him about the place called Cheddar's so he'd decided to take her there. Judging by the crowd that was sitting outside of the building, the food had to be just as good as Demoto had told him. Since there were so many people crowding the entrance and foyer of the restaurant, Uzoma let Jocelynn's hand go once they were next to the small bench and walked ahead of her to put their names on the list.

He told her she could sit down and wait on him near the water fountain before walking away. He looked at all of the people waiting and watching him like he was some sort of fish in a bowl as he gave the hostess their name.

"Bitchhhh, fine as hell," some lady from beside him said.

Uzoma didn't bother to pay that any attention because he assumed that conversation had nothing to do with him until he heard the second girl.

"You ain't never lied. I would be fucking his fine ass every second of the damn day. Pulling all over them dreads"

His nose instantly began to twitch as he listened to the women talk so openly disgusting about him. It was such a turn off for a woman to act and speak that way in public.

"Excuse me, sir," one of them tried to get his attention as he turned to walk away.

Uzoma looked their way, but said nothing.

"You single?" the first one asked before they both started laughing.

Uzoma didn't even render an answer. He turned back around and headed back to Jocelynn. When he got outside she was looking out at the street watching the cars pass by. He sat down smoothly next to her and leaned over, resting his forearms on his knees.

"They said the wait was about ten minutes."

Joc nodded, but didn't say anything.

"You straight?" he asked when he noticed that she wasn't smiling or anything.

"Yeah. I'm fine."

She could lie to somebody else, but he knew her better than that. Uzoma turned to look at her. "Look at me, Jocelynn."

She shook her head no and kept looking at her feet. Uzoma definitely knew something was wrong then.

"Jocelynn, I won't tell you again. Look at me when I'm speaking to you."

Joc turned her head slowly, avoiding eye contact as long as she could before looking at him.

"Tell me what's wrong with you."

"Nothing."

"Don't lie again. Tell me."

She huffed and looked away but must have remembered he'd

246

just told her to look at him, because she turned her head right back around.

"Why you let my hand go and leave me out here?" Her voice was quiet, but he'd heard her. "You didn't want me to go with you?

"Nah, I left you because I didn't want you trying to maneuver through all of those people. Plus, you already told me you didn't feel well. I didn't want you to be standing up for no reason."

"I could have went with you."

"Well, I'm sorry, bae, I honestly wasn't thinking about it like that." He sat up and wrapped his arm around her neck. "You forgive me?"

She nodded.

"Well give me a kiss so I'll know you ain't lying."

Joc kissed his lips, but he could tell that there was something still bothering her.

"You don't forgive me,"

"Yes I do, it's just…"

"Just what?"

"I saw you talking to those other women. Do you know them?"

Uzoma reprimanded himself for not knowing better than letting her hand go and talking to other women in her presence. Even if he really hadn't said anything to them. Jocelynn was sensitive, and even more so since she'd been pregnant.

"Those hoes were tacky as fuck. I didn't even say anything to them."

Joc nodded her head. "I believe you."

"Youngblood, party of two." Sounded throughout the small waiting area before Uzoma could say anything else to her.

This time, when he stood to his feet to go inside, he grabbed her hand and helped her up. Once she was on her feet and about to walk

248

past him he stepped behind her and wrapped both of his hands around her waist. He held her close to him as he began walking awkwardly with her in his arms.

"What are you doing?" He could hear the smile in her voice.

"Making sure the world knows who you belong to. It's a lot of niggas up in here. I don't want them getting the wrong idea."

Joc giggled bashfully as he kissed all over the side of her face. "Um huh, you need to be doing this for all these women that keep staring at you."

"Fuck them," he told her nastily.

When they got inside, the same group of women were in the same spot. He could see them eyeing him and Joc as they passed through the waiting area, so he made sure to be a little extra with Joc, touching and tickling her stomach. She was so busy laughing and enjoying the attention that he was giving her that she hadn't even noticed the evil looks the women were giving her.

Uzoma made sure to shoot their asses a look that was much more deadly than the little shit they thought they were putting off. If they thought Joc was open for any ill feelings, they had no idea who they were fucking with. He would give those hoes the business straight the fuck up. He didn't give a fuck if they were women.

The small booth they were seated in was right in the open of the whole restaurant. There were people and plants all around them. The atmosphere was nice and calming, Uzoma could get with it. He looked across the table at Jocelynn, who was scanning through the menu casually, not looking very enthused.

"You don't see anything you like?"

She looked up at him and shook her head. "Not yet. You?"

"Hell yeah, I see something I like. I wish I could get me a lil taste of it right now, but this ain't even the place for that, baby." He rubbed his hands together dramatically while shaking his head from side to side.

Joc was smiling so hard, he could see all of her teeth as she looked away from him before returning her gaze back to him.

"Yo nasty ass. You should have got some before we left the house. You was so busy watching me do my hair, you should have been getting your little fix then. I could have bust it open for you real quick."

Uzoma laughed at her because he'd already known she was going to play right into his joke. Joc was just as nasty as him. Sometimes nastier. That's why she was his baby. She equaled him out in ways he didn't even know he needed. He remembered Lu telling him she was going to change him, had no idea back then just how true that would one day be.

"How are you two? I'm Pricilla, I'll be your server today. Can I start you off with something to drink?"

Uzoma could see Joc in his peripheral looking over at him. Something she always did when they went out. She loved to eat, but she'd learned to let him take the lead when it came to ordering their

251

food. It wasn't anything he made her do, it was just something the submissive part of her preferred he take care of.

"I'll have sweet tea, and you can her a strawberry lemonade."

The server smiled and nodded at him before walking away. While they waited for her to come back, they made small talk about their babies and what they were going to name them. Joc had been so caught up in their conversation that she hadn't even decided what she was going to eat.

"You still don't know what you want?"

"Not really."

Uzoma asked the waitress to give them another few minutes before she walked away.

"I think I want the pasta, but I kind of want the steak and shrimp. I don't know though, because that may be too much food."

"I don't think so. You can eat it. Just get the steak." Uzoma tried to help her out.

252

Joc was quiet as she continued looking at the menu. When the waitress came back, Uzoma ordered her the steak and the ribs and fries for himself. She took their menus and left just as quickly as she'd come. Once they were alone again, Uzoma looked back at Jocelynn, preparing to have a conversation with her, but was stopped by the tears in her ears.

He looked at her utterly confused as to what the problem could have been right then. They hadn't done anything but order food. Nothing else had happened.

"Jocelynn?"

She sniffed hard and wiped at her eyes. "Huh?"

"Baby, what is the problem now?" He sounded extremely confused.

"You keep trying to make me fat."

Uzoma's eyes blinked rapidly as he stared at her in disbelief.

"Come again?"

253

"You keep trying to make me fat. You said it at home that you hope I keep the weight I've gained, and just now you said I could eat the steak and shrimp right after I said it was too much food. Like I'm just some cow or something." She rolled her eyes as she spoke. "You can't keep just feeding me to make me how you like me, Uzoma. I don't want to be fat." She started crying again. "That's why you brought me here. You're always feeding me. Every day, that's all you do," Joc continued to rant.

Uzoma, on the other hand, sat back in his seat watching her, trying to figure if she serious or not, because he was hoping like hell that she wasn't. One minute they were good, laughing and playing, and the next, she was crying about something.

"Them babies got your ass fucked up." He couldn't even suppress the laughter that erupted from him mouth. "You need to hurry up and have them because you're losing your gotdamn mind."

"Ain't nothing wrong with me. That's you. You keep feeding me so I can get fat. If you wanted a fat girl then you should have got one, hell," she called herself fussing at him.

Uzoma leaned forward and looked at her. "Jocelynn, do you realize how crazy you sound right now, baby? You sitting in a restaurant telling me that I'm feeding you too much." He waved his hand around in the air. "What else are you supposed to do here, baby? Huh? Tell me so we can do it." The humor was laced all through his voice as he sat across from her smiling.

Joc sucked her teeth. "You know what. Just don't worry about it. You always trying to be funny with your ole African ass." She crossed her arms over her chest in a huff. "Just don't say nothing else to me."

Uzoma really started laughing then. "Man, Joc, you are cutting up, girl."

"Oh, so now I'm Joc?" She bit her bottom lip as it started trembling.

Uzoma could already see the new tears forming, so he got up and hurried around to her side and wrapped his arm around her shoulder.

"No you're not, Joc... Jocelynn, you're my baby. How about that?" He snickered as he rubbed up and down her shoulder. "You like that better?"

"You're going to feed me steak until I'm big as house then you're going to leave." She sniffed hard. "That's all you're going to do. Just make me a fucking cow, why don't you? All of my clothes are already getting too small, my buttons won't button, and all you do is give me food," she ranted as Uzoma did his best to hold in his laugh.

"Can I get you two anyth—" The waitress stopped and looked at Joc. "Is she okay?"

"Yes, she'—" Uzoma was about to answer for her, but Joc interrupted him.

"Yes, I'm fine! And I wanted pasta, not steak!" She damn near yelled at the lady.

The slight frown in the woman's forehead didn't go unnoticed by Uzoma, but all he could do was smile and shake his head.

"I'm sorry about that, ma'am. She's pregnant and can't control herself right now. Is it too late to get her the pasta?"

"I can control myself," Joc sassed making Uzoma and the server chuckle.

Uzoma returned his attention to the server. "Can she have the pasta? She's afraid if she eats the steak she'll turn into a cow."

Joc elbowed him so hard in his side that he coughed. He and the waitress both laughed before she told him she would fix Joc's order.

"Can you bring her some bread or something while we wait too, please? She's not herself when she's hungry," he told the lady, copying off of the popular Snickers commercial.

He and the server were laughing as Joc sat next to him rolling her eyes and mumbling stuff to herself about him and the waitress being stupid and inconsiderate.

"You better stop cutting up, girl." He kissed her forehead. "In this place acting like you ain't got no damn sense."

"Well, if you would stop trying to talk about me to the little dumb waitress."

Uzoma looked down at her and kissed the top of her head. His boys had her showing her ass on the regular, and on most days, it was so funny he could hardly comfort her. Much like right then. Her crying and mood swings should have been something on America's Funniest Home Videos or something.

A couple of hours passed before they'd gotten done eating and was on their way home from the restaurant. While he was driving, Uzoma called and told him that their friends, Jacko and Kia, were coming over to play cards, and for him and Joc to come too.

Joc was all for it until he told her that Kia and Jacko would be there. She'd never met Jacko, but she hadn't really been feeling Kia since their first encounter, and that was his fault.

"Listen, I'm telling you now, my nigga, if you don't want me to show my ass up in here, don't play with me. I better not catch you and Kia doing none of that flirting stuff y'all was doing the other night or I'm going off in both of y'all shit, you hear me?" Every ounce of Brooklyn that Joc had in her oozed out in that one statement. From the accent to the lingo.

"Calm down, baby. I told you it wasn't like that the first time. Plus, this girl's husband is going to be in here."

Joc turned in her seat to look at him. "You think I give a fuck about what it wasn't like or the fact that her nigga will be in there? Hell no. I will still slap you and her. You feel me?"

Uzoma blew her a kiss instead of answering.

"Okay, I see you think I'm playing. Just try me." Joc opened the door and prepared to get out. "Come help me get out of this little ass car," she yelled at him.

Uzoma watched her with a smile on his face before she yelled for him to come help her again, so he got out. The entire walk up the sidewalk, he watched the way her hips and ass moved with every step she took. She could complain all day about that weight, but he was in love with it.

She was so fucking juicy he could hardly keep his eyes off her. "Man, Jocelynn, listen to your man when I tell you ain't nobody fucking with you, baby. You fine as hell."

She looked over her shoulder and smiled at him just as he pressed his body into hers so that she could feel how hard he was getting just by looking at her.

"You be doing this shit, man. I just be chilling, then you bring your sexy ass around and my dick just goes crazy." He was licking her neck and rubbing his hand up the front of her thigh when the front door opened.

Joc tried to step out of his grasp, but he pulled her back to him before looking up to see who was standing in the door. It was Taryn's big belly ass. She had her hair up into one of those big ponytails like the ones Joc always put hers in, and some tights and a Double O T-shirt.

"Do y'all have to do that at other people's house?" she playfully sassed as she stepped to the side so that they could walk in.

"That was this nigga. I was minding my own business." Joc pointed over her shoulder at Uzoma once they were inside the house.

Taryn looked him up and down with a smirk on her face. "I know it was. Nasty ass, just like Demoto."

Versus saying anything to the women, Uzoma just smiled and walked behind them into the living room. There was already music playing and voices could be heard before they even rounded the corner. When they finally got into the living room, Uzoma dapped Demoto and Jacko up before saying what's up to Kia and sitting down at the table where they were playing cards.

"Y'all got next," Jacko told them. "We beating Taryn and Demoto's ass already."

"Because of Moto's nonplaying ass." Taryn slid her cards down on the table.

Uzoma and Joc made themselves comfortable in the other chairs around the table as the conversations continued. Everyone was laughing and playing, having a good time as the hours passed. Before long Uzoma, Jacko, and Demoto were all on the verge of being drunk. They'd been drinking and playing cards well after the girls had decided to bail and just talk.

"Aye, baby, can you bring me some more ice out the kitchen?" Uzoma looked at Joc.

She nodded and stood from where she was sitting and headed into the kitchen. When she passed by him, he slapped her butt hard and started rapping and singing to her.

"Fine as hell, thick is as fuck... oh my god! That's my baby!"

He slurred drunkenly.

Everybody in the room started laughing, even Joc as he did his best version of the verse from the song "Caroline."

"Shut up, Uzoma, with your drunk ass." Her face blushed as she giggled.

"Just hurry up with my ice, Caroline!" he yelled behind her again.

"Man, I remember when this nigga was begging me to find him a wife like me when we were in Cameroon. Now he sitting here in love. Time goes by too fast." Taryn was smiling at him as she told everybody about Uzoma.

"It's obvious, too. Look at how he be watching her," Kia chimed in busting him out.

He had indeed been watching Jocelynn. As soon as she walked back around the corner with his cup of ice, her breasts had caught his eye, and he'd been practically drooling at the mouth ever since.

263

Lust was seeping through every pore on his body as he bit his bottom lip.

"Shawty fine as fuck. I don't be trying to be all in love like these two niggas." He pointed at Jacko and Demoto. "It's just hard as hell not to be." He smiled lazily as his hand grazed the back of Joc's thighs when she stopped next to him.

"I love you too." She kissed his waiting lips before returning to where she'd been sitting with Taryn and Kia.

As the night went on, they all eventually gravitated into the living room and were occupying some part of the sofa's or floors. Demoto and Taryn were laid back on the sofa, while Jacko sat with his back against the sofa and Kia rested between his legs.

He was stretched out in the recliner with Jocelynn sitting on his lap. She'd tried to sit next to him, but he was feeling nasty and wanted to feel her on his dick. Since they were in a room full of people, that was the best he could do right then.

"Joc, you and Uzoma are so cute," Taryn swooned.

"Thank you. We're just trying to be like y'all," she replied with Uzoma's hand twirling her hair.

"Girl, ain't we all." Kia laughed. "The Youngbloods are marriage goals, honey."

"Girl please, y'all don't want these problems. Demoto be having me about to kill his ass every day."

Kia looked over her shoulder at Jacko. "Jack, you know about that, don't you?"

Jacko covered her mouth with his hand before biting her neck. "That's your disobedient ass."

"Oh my goodness. I remember when I heard y'all fucking in that bathroom at that Double O mansion party that night, and Jacko called your ass disobedient," Taryn squealed. "Bitch, I died. I knew my Jacky boy was the truth after that. He gets your ass in line."

The room erupted in laughter as Kia covered her face. "You

mean that party that you was stripping at after Demoto told your ass to quit?" Kia placed her finger behind her ear dramatically. "You talking about that one?"

Taryn rolled her eyes. "Bitch, you ain't have to say that."

"Taryn, you used to strip?" Joc asked in disbelief.

"Yeah, she tried it before I ended it. She knew better than to try me." Demoto looked serious as hell as he pushed some of his hair from his face.

"That's right, Moto. Bitch talking about me, Demoto don't play with your muthafuckin' ass. Bitch ain't stripping no more. Barefoot and pregnant. That's this hoe's whole life now." Kia, Taryn, and Joc all burst out laughing.

"I don't know what you laughing at, Jocelynn," Uzoma said lazily from behind her.

Kia and Taryn giggled even harder, both ready for some more straightening.

"She be trying to be on some ole slick shit, but this dick get her right every time." Uzoma pushed his hips upward into her butt.

"Get her." Jacko laughed.

"Make her ass join the club," Demoto said as he rubbed Taryn's large stomach. "I could tell the first night I met her that she likes to be on bullshit. Barefoot and pregnant, bruh." He winked at Joc when Uzoma told them all that was his plan.

Late into the night, all of them sat around laughing and talking. It was well into the wee hours of the morning when Joc excused herself to go to the bathroom. Uzoma sat in the recliner as long as he could, but that liquor had his dick hard, and watching Joc walk away hadn't helped any.

Everybody else was wrapped up doing their own thing and watching TV, so he eased up behind her and walked down the hallway. She had just opened the door when he got to the bathroom, so it was easy for him to push her back inside and close the door behind him.

"Boy, what are you doing?" She looked at him with a raised eyebrow.

"Finna get me some of this pussy." He grabbed her and pulled her to him forcefully while kissing her lips and groping her butt.

"Not here like this. Everybody is going to know what we're back here doing." She tried to push him away with no success.

Uzoma looked at her like she was crazy. "I don't give a fuck." He rolled down the stretchy part of her maternity pants. "You ain't about to tell me no to some ass that belongs to me." He sucked on the side of her neck. "Especially on the account of other people." He pushed her pants down and snatched them off one of her legs and pulled her back to him. "I dun told you about that shit."

Uzoma's locs fell around his shoulders and into his face as he stared at her lustfully. Though she was no longer saying anything, he could tell she wanted to, but it was time out for that shit. She could tell him what she thought and how she didn't want to fuck in somebody else's house after his first nut. He might be more open to listen after that, but right then, he wasn't trying to hear the shit.

"They gon' hear me," she whined. "You know you be going too hard sometimes," she whimpered as he dropped down to his knees in front of her.

"Let them hear you then, baby." Uzoma pushed her back into the counter and propped her leg up on his shoulder before leaning forward and covering her slippery wet opening with his mouth. He sucked it slowly before placing a sloppy kiss on it. "Let 'em here what I do to you."

Joc's head had fallen back as she held herself steady on the counter. Uzoma was licking and sucking every part of her love that he could. He was so turned on by just the smell of her, that when she began to release low moans, it felt like his dick was about to explode. Her pussy in his mouth had been on his mind all night, and he was finally getting some.

Uzoma was like a bad crack fiend when it came to Jocelynn's

269

body. No matter how much they indulged in sex, he couldn't get enough. Once he felt he'd had enough to hold him off until they got home, he stood to his feet and pushed his jeans down.

Joc sat on the counter eyeing him hungrily. As soon as he was ready, he snatched her to the edge of the counter, wrapping both of her legs around his waist before rubbing the head of his dick around her sticky essence, and just like it always did, his dick found its way home.

Slowly, it slid deeper and deeper until he'd tortured himself enough and plunged deep inside of her. "Fuckkkk!" He gritted his teeth as her walls tightened around him. "Mmmmmh," he moaned into her ear when he leaned forward. "Dammit, Jocelynn."

Uzoma closed his eyes and lost himself in her. She was so warm and inviting as her thighs held him close to her body. The sounds coming from her mouth and her pussy had him so zoned out that he had started moaning louder than her.

"Sshhh, they're going to hear you."

Uzoma barely opened his eyes as he kissed up and down her neck. "I don't care. Let them hear what you do to me." His lips grazed her ear just as she grabbed his face and covered his mouth with hers.

"I love you." She pulled at his bottom lip. "I fucking love you." Joc began kissing all over his face until she got down to his neck.

Her tongue slid methodically over his Adam's apple, making his knees weak. Uzoma had already been teetering on the edge of his orgasm when she told him that she loved him, but now that she was kissing and touching all over him, he was about to fall straight over and bust.

"Come on, baby, get yours," he grunted into her ear.

Joc scooted closer to him and widened her legs so that he could hit her spot. Her long hair dangled behind her as he held her body in his arms. Her perfectly beautiful face was squinted tightly as she fought with the pleasure from his dick.

271

"Look at me when you cum, Jocelynn," he commanded as he deepened his strokes.

Joc's eyes opened immediately, sucking him in further. Uzoma winked before blowing her a kiss. Moments later, her legs were shaking in his arms and her breathing was labored as she tried to catch her breath.

Uzoma looked down between him at all of the creamy white substance coating his erection. "Damn, that's some sweet loving, girl."

Joc's face was somber as she watched him until he finished. Uzoma fell over on top of her, trying to gather his strength as he released himself inside of her. It felt like he would never stop cumming. When he was finally able to pull himself away from her, he wet a few paper towels and cleaned herself up before wiping his dick and stuffing it back into his underwear.

He was sure to help her from the counter and back into her jeans before looking around the bathroom to make sure everything was good. Joc looked sleepy as she stood in the middle of the floor waiting for him. He grabbed her hand and was about to turn the knob, but she stopped him.

"Everybody is going to know." She smiled brightly.

He shrugged. "They need to know."

She was still smiling and shaking her head as they exited the bathroom. Uzoma made sure to stand in front of her when they entered the living room so that he would get the bulk of the attention. Just like Joc had tried to warn him, they were all looking at him with some sort of smile or look of amusement on their faces.

"I hope y'all cleaned up behind y'allselves. That's my baby's bathroom. He don't need to accidentally slip on none of y'all juices." Taryn didn't even wait for them to sit down before she started talking.

"All that damn noise. Save that shit for y'all house," Kia egged her on.

273

"That pregnant pussy ain't no hoe, is it, nigga?" Demoto shot Uzoma a sly smirk. "I know that was your ass doing all that damn cussing and moaning."

"Boy!" Uzoma bucked his eyes as he rubbed his hands together.

"Aye, don't feel bad, my nigga. When Kia was pregnant, I was diving in that shit anywhere I could get it." Jacko shook his head as he thought about what he was saying.

"Jocelynn, bring your ass around this boy so we can see your lil freaky behind," Kia told her.

"Ain't no point in being shame now. We're all nasty as hell. We can't judge nobody." Taryn tried to ease her nervousness.

They all chilled and made joke after joke well into the morning before they eventually fell asleep. Uzoma was cuddled in the large recliner with Joc asleep on his lap while he rubbed her stomach. He watched her sleep for a few minutes before he too drifted off with everyone else.

Chapter 10: Never knew I needed you

The light breeze coming off the water brushed against Zino's face at the same time the smell of it wafted up his nose, making him aware of the beach they were near. It was midafternoon, and he and Lonnie had landed in Virginia almost two hours before.

Somehow, he had allowed her to talk him into finally going to visit Phoenix. At first, he'd been so upset with her for calling without his permission that he hadn't spoken for an entire week, but after thinking about it and realizing that she had only been trying to help, his anger eased enough for him to apologize and make things back right with them.

Lonnie, being the understanding person that she was, brushed it off and immediately booked their flights to Virginia. She'd been talking off and on to Phoenix since then, sometimes while he was

275

right next to her, and not one time had she given him the opportunity to talk to her.

Not that he wanted to or anything, it was just funny to him how comfortable she and Phoenix had gotten with each other. Clearly, she had been right when she said everybody loved her, because the Phoenix he knew would never attach herself to another female like that. Especially now, after what had happened with Tone and the last female she'd befriended.

"You sure you ready?" Lonnie raised her eyebrow at him.

They had just gotten out of their rental car at the address that Phoenix had given Lonnie. Upon getting to Virginia, they'd gone to their hotel and dropped their things off and had sex. Zino was too wound up and needed to relieve himself some before he allowed his mind and body to get the best of him.

Like he'd known it would before sliding into it, Lonnie's body had put him in the appropriate headspace for his meeting. He was no longer tense or nervous. He was actually a lot calmer than he'd expected to be. Lonnie's presence was helping out a lot as well.

"Yeah, I'm good." He took the hand she had stretched out toward him and they walked up the stairs together.

Lonnie gave his hand a light squeeze before ringing the doorbell. The sound of the doorbell must have had an invisible trigger connected to his heart because he instantly began to get nervous again. Though it wasn't noticeable, his legs and arms had even begun to tremble.

When he heard the locks clicking, he thought his knees would buckle, but the strangest thing happened. The moment he saw Phoenix, every nerve relaxed. She looked the exact same, still small, and still as beautiful as ever. Her hair had grown out, and she'd added a few pounds, but she was still his twin.

The tears in her eyes and the smile on her face made him think about the old days. She was so happy to see him that she nearly broke down the screen door that separated them. When she was finally able to get it open, she bum rushed him and wrapped her arms around his neck.

Instinctively, he hugged her to him with just as much feeling. They stood hugging one another for at least a good five minutes before Phoenix pulled away, only to grab right back onto him. Having Phoenix in his arms and in his life again made all of his pain go away.

It was crazy how he hadn't known just how much stress he'd been holding onto by not contacting her. Being near her and thinking of the life they all used to share made him feel like he could breathe again. For the past few months, he had been going through life doing whatever it took to make it to the next day, trying not to think of the only family he'd known, and it had taken a major toll on him.

"Look at you, twin," Phoenix spoke through her tears once she'd pulled away for the second time. "You look so good, Z."

"You too, sis." Zino looked at Phoenix's tear stained face before pulling her in for another hug. "I missed you."

"I missed you so much too, Zino. What took you so long to find me? I told your ass before you went upstate that I was going to be waiting on you when you got out." Phoenix punched him in the chest. "You make me sick being so stupid." She punched him again in the same spot.

Zino chuckled lightly. "Lil feisty ass." He grinned. "I see ain't shit changed. You ain't my mama, Fe."

She frowned at him. "I don't care about being your mama. I'm your sister, you should have hit me up, Zino. You were all I had." The latter part of her sentence sounded a little wounded, and it made him feel bad.

They were both quiet for a minute, just looking at each other and not saying anything. She was right. He was, and he'd let her down.

"I'm sorry, Fe, I was just going through a lot mentally."

"And still is," Lonnie sidelined.

279

Hearing her voice made Zino smile. He'd been so wrapped up in Phoenix, he'd momentarily forgotten she was there. He and Phoenix looked at her at the same time with smiles on their faces. Lonnie held her hand up in mock defense.

"I'm just saying, sir, you're still a little jacked up in the head, so don't say you was, say you are."

Zino and Phoenix both snickered at her attempt at lightening the mood.

"Well, twin, I guess I'm still pretty fucked up." Zino looked back at Phoenix.

"Well ,that makes two of us," She looked off into the distance for a minute before looking back at him. "Y'all come on in the house." She stepped out of the way and ushered them inside her home.

It smelled like cinnamon and something else Zino couldn't place, but it was nice as hell, and big. It was decorated in the typical

Phoenix manner, and extremely comfortable. He saw a baby playpen in the living room they were passing through, along with a few pink blankets.

"Fe, how many kids you got?"

"Two. A boy and a girl."

"Damn," Zino said more to himself than anything. He really had missed a lot. "Where they daddy?"

"I'm right here. Who's asking?" A tall bald headed man walked into the room holding a baby girl in his arms.

When he saw Zino and Lonnie, he smiled and extended his hand toward them both. Zino shook it with Lonnie following.

"Jamison."

Zino's eyes squinted for a minute as he stared at the man. Something about him looked familiar, he just couldn't place it.

"He's Tone's friend."

Zino snapped in realization when Phoenix helped him understand. "I knew I knew him."

Jamison gave another friendly smile. "I've been taking care of her. It's a hard job, but she's been straight since she got out."

"I appreciate that, fam." Zino looked from Jamison to Phoenix before she told him and Lonnie to come into the dining room because she'd just finished cooking.

They all settled around the dining room table to eat before engaging in conversation again.

"Lonnie, I can't thank you enough for this." Phoenix looked like she wanted to cry again as she watched Zino eat.

"Girl, he needed you. He's been going crazy without you. I'm really big on family, so I've been trying to get him to connect back with you for a while. I'm just glad he finally agreed."

"Me and twin have always been the most stubborn. Tone used to get so mad with us because neither of us ever did what he said without a fight. That's how we ended up being called twins. We were the youngest two of the Zoo Crew, and we acted just alike. We liked to party, hang out, and do young kid shit, while Bear, Tek, and Tone was about their business." Phoenix smiled as she thought about the old days.

"Not Tek. That nigga was reckless as fuck. I don't know who kept us in the most shit, you or him," Zino joined in on her walk down memory lane.

Phoenix laughed and hit the table, scaring her baby. The baby began to cry, but Jamison rocked her back to sleep so that Phoenix could enjoy herself.

"Man, what? Tek was the worst one, but my boy just wanted to have fun. He was just a young nigga enjoying the place he was in. That's all." Her voice broke.

Zino cleared his throat and stopped eating as he watched Phoenix cry. Clearly thinking about their past was just as painful for her as it was for him.

"Don't cry, Fe, we had good times, sis."

She sniffed and tried to wipe her face, but it was useless, her tears weren't stopping. Lonnie must have felt that Zino was on the verge of his own breakdown because she was up out of her seat and sitting on his lap at the same time that Jamison had leaned over and wrapped his arm around Phoenix.

Lonnie's arms being around his neck as her cheek rested on the top of his head made Zino feel so much better. She was so warm and comforting. Without even knowing it, Lonnie had become his safe haven. She was the one thing who took away any and everything that he was feeling. She replaced his storms with sunlight.

The thought of her alone had his arms circling her small body. He held her close to him as he nuzzled his face into her breasts. He didn't want the tears to come, but they were inevitable. They weren't as heavy as Phoenix's, but they were there. He cried only for a few seconds before pulling his face back and looking across the table at Phoenix.

She was lying with her head against Jamison's chest, looking exhausted as ever. She was no longer crying, but she was still sniffling, trying to gain control of her feelings.

"I'm so happy you're here, Zino."

"Me too, Fe."

"How long are y'all staying?"

"I packed me and this nut job enough clothes for a week,"

Phoenix, Jamison, and Zino all laughed at Lonnie. She was seriously the light of his life.

"Man, this talking ass girl will say anything, so don't pay her ass no attention." Zino bit the side of her face, making her blush and giggle.

"How long have y'all been together?" Jamison asked.

Lonnie's face frowned immediately. "We ain't together. He don't want me like that. He just wants to play games."

"Now, Zino…" Everything about Phoenix's tone let him know that she was about to go off in one of those girly rants, telling him why he needed to be with Lonnie and how she was good for him and blah blah blah.

"Hush, Fe, she's a liar. She know she my girlfriend."

Lonnie leaned back so she could see his face. "Nigga, since when?"

"Since I gave you this dick. Hell you talking about since when?"

"Oh my god!" Lonnie covered her face in embarrassment. "Y'all excuse his mouth."

Phoenix and Jamison were both laughing when Phoenix spoke. "Twin been like that forever. That nigga ain't never had no sense."

"It's so embarrassing."

Zino kissed Lonnie's face as she continued to tell Jamison and Phoenix all about him. She and Phoenix had even taken the conversation to a more serious one, talking about his breakdown at her mom's house and the cemetery. That conversation eventually turned into one with her and Jamison.

He too shared all of the stuff he'd endured during Phoenix's grieving process. The four of them and the baby stayed at the table for almost two hours, just talking and catching up before moving into the living room. They settled down and took things to a lighter note.

"So, how often can I expect visits, Zino?"

Zino looked at Phoenix. "Why you can't come visit me?"

"I can. I'm just making sure you ain't gon' leave here and I never see your ass again."

He shook his head. "Nah, that won't ever happen again."

"Better not."

Zino and Lonnie stayed for another few hours with Phoenix and Jamison, catching up on life before going back to their hotel room. It was approaching eleven o'clock at night when they finally walked

287

into their room. Zino didn't know about Lonnie, but he was tired as hell.

After all that traveling, eating, and crying, he'd worn himself out. He was ready for a shower and the bed. He made sure the locks on the door was locked before walking deeper into the room to look for Lonnie. He didn't see her, but he heard the shower.

He stripped down quickly before joining her in the bathroom. She was already in the shower and lathered up with soap when he stepped in behind her. She stepped forward some to give him some room, but he pulled her back to him. Her back to his chest.

He kissed her shoulder and just held onto her. "Thank you."

"No thanks needed." She continued rubbing soap onto her hands and arms.

"You really want an abandoned, ex-murderer, motherless orphan turned mentally unstable nutcase as your boyfriend?"

"You used to murder people?"

Zino nodded, afraid of what she was about to say.

"Will you murder me?"

"Fuck no."

"Well then, yes. I'll take your problem having ass to be my lawfully wedded boyfriend." She giggled, using his lingo.

Zino's laughter merged with hers as they stood in the shower together. He held on to her as if she was about to leave him at any second, but she wasn't moving, so that was a good enough sign for him.

"You like me for real, huh?"

She sucked her teeth. "If you can't tell that by now, then you're blind."

"Not blind, just unsure. Most of the time when people tell me they love me and I actually accept them into my life, they always die, so it takes me a while to see when people are genuine enough to stay."

Lonnie was quiet as she spun around in his arms. She rubbed his shoulders, wiping the excess soap from her hands on him while looking into his eyes.

"I wouldn't leave you."

"I don't have anybody except Phoenix,"

"You have me and my family. My mama loves you."

Zino smiled as he thought of what her mama must think of him. "I love her too."

"We can share her if you want. I don't mind sharing my family with you, Zino, and they're not going anywhere. They love me and you too. Probably more now than before because they know you have problems, and for some reason, they like to fix people." She rolled her eyes. "But they're yours if you want them."

Zino liked the thought of sharing her family. As crazy as it seemed, he actually wanted that. They were all very nice people and would probably be some of the best people he would ever connect to.

"What about you, though?"

Lonnie looked confused. "What about me?"

"Are you mine if I want you?"

"Of course," she told him without thinking.

Zino loved her more in that moment than he'd ever loved any woman. Who would have thought sitting up in that hospital all day watching Maverick's lowdown ass would lead him to the love and happiness he'd been absentmindedly hoping for his entire life? Life had a funny way of working things out, but he was happy that it had decided to give him a break, and one final chance at love.

Chapter 11: What's it like to be in love?

The sun was shining brightly as the cold months were finally wrapping up. It was the first week of May, and Jocelynn and Uzoma had just left the mall shopping for Dakeyo and Deumi. After hearing Taryn and Demoto's kids' names, Jocelynn wanted the twins to have a piece of their father's heritage as well.

Uzoma, being the same thoughtful man she'd known since she met him, promised her that he would think of some Cameroonian names for the boys. It had taken him nearly two months because he wanted to pick something good and fitting. Once he finally told her the two he'd chosen, her heart melted and they'd stuck ever since.

So far, everything in her pregnancy had been going wonderfully, and the twins would be there in a few short months. She had gotten a lot bigger, and couldn't wait for the day that her body was free of tiny humans again. It was exhausting, and she felt like a whale. Although Uzoma made sure to let her know how much he loved her appearance, she needed to get back right for herself.

"You hungry?" Uzoma squeezed her hand softly.

"Yes, you?"

He rubbed his stomach. "Hell yeah. Let's go to Longhorn. I want some steak."

"Fine with me. You want to call Lu and Brasi, or are they still at her physical therapy appointment?"

Uzoma shrugged. "Last time I talked to them, that's where they were."

"Well let's just go by ourselves. I'd rather be alone with you anyway."

Uzoma let her hand go and wrapped his arm around her shoulder, drawing her closer to his body. "You read my mind."

They'd traveled to visit Lu, Brasi, and Zino for a few days since it had been a minute since they'd seen everybody, and because Uzoma was the best man in Zino's wedding the next day. Though Jocelynn hadn't gotten the chance to really get to know Zino any more than the little time she'd spent with everybody when she first visited Lu all those months ago, she was truly happy for him.

He was such a sweet and cool person, and him finding happiness was very dear to her heart. Not to mention how happy Uzoma was. He was always telling her how hard life had been for Zino, so when Zino called and told Uzoma that his girlfriend was making him have a wedding, and that he wanted him to be his best man, she wasn't the least bit surprised by his reaction. He was overjoyed.

You would have thought he was the one getting married by the way he was acting. It had only been three months since Zino had gone to visit his family in Virginia, and Uzoma had relayed to her how much he'd changed since then, and from the few times she'd talked to him over the phone, she could tell it was the truth.

"What time y'all have to be at the church tomorrow?" Joc asked as they walked through the doors of the restaurant.

"I think he said ten." Uzoma smiled as he did whenever the wedding was mentioned. "I can't believe this nigga is really about to get married."

"Why not? Everybody has got to grow up someday."

"I know, I'm just saying, Zino used to stay wilding out, and now he finna' settle down for life." Uzoma laughed more to himself than anything.

"Well, you can't hoe around all your life,"

Uzoma looked over at her and nudged her shoulder with his. "I know, that ain't what I meant. All it takes is the right woman, and any man can be changed."

"Only if he's ready to be changed."

Uzoma nodded in agreement as the hostess finally came to seat them. Jocelynn followed close behind him as they headed to their table. She was minding her business and thinking about how good that bread and butter was about to be when she heard somebody calling her name.

When she turned around to see who it was, it was the last person she would have ever expected. "Mom?"

She hadn't talked to her in so long, that she'd totally forgotten that her mother even lived there. Lu had been the only person she'd visited in Georgia for so long that her mother never even came to mind. Jocelynn followed her mother with her eyeballs as she walked up on her.

She still looked the same as she did so many years ago, just with gray hair. Her face held a smug look as she approached, already putting Joc in a sour mood. She was in no mood for the foolishness that followed her mother whenever she was around.

"I thought that was you when you walked in."

Joc nodded and reached for a hug. Her mother gave her a quick hug before looking over at Uzoma, who was ushering them out of the middle of the floor and over into the corner so they could talk.

"So, it's safe to assume he's the reason for this?" she asked, pointing at Joc's stomach.

"Yes, ma'am. That would be me." Uzoma extended his hand in her direction. "Uzoma Youngblood."

Her mother took his hand before looking over at Joc with questioning eyes. "Foreign?" She nodded. "Good choice."

"Thanks," Joc responded dryly. She was still stuck on the comment her mother had made about her babies. The hell she meant by *this*? Her babies weren't no damn *this*. They were kids, and they were hers.

"You're big, girl! I was never that big with you."

Joc's eyes rolled. "That's because I'm having twins."

Her mother covered her mouth. "Oh, Jocelynn!" She touched

297

the side of Joc's body, picking up the extra skin there. "You are going to have to work super hard to get that weigh off you."

Uzoma snaked his hand around Joc's neck possessively with a frown on his face before kissing her temple. "I think she looks beautiful pregnant. If she never loses a pound, she'll still be the most beautiful woman on the planet."

Her mother looked him up and down before turning her nose up at him. "Never loses a pound, huh?" She looked at Jocelynn with a look of disdain. "You better not listen to him, girl, all men want you to do is get fat so nobody else will want you. You better come up off that weight."

"Mam—" Jocelynn started, but was cut off by Uzoma.

"I'm sorry you feel that way about me, ma'am, but if you think you're about to stand here and continue to insult Jocelynn, then you can be on your way."

"Excuse you? Be on my way?" She frowned at him. "I don't

know how Jocelynn lets you talk to her, but I don't take orders from no man."

"That's clear. However, as Jocelynn's man, my job is to protect her, and that means from anybody. So, like I stated a moment ago, you can keep the insults." He was quiet for a minute, giving her time to digest what he'd just said. "I won't repeat myself."

The commanding tone sent shivers down Joc's spine, so she knew her mother was probably shaking in her little Payless heels.

"Whatever, little boy. Jocelynn, it was good to see you. I guess this is the best I can do since you never make your way anywhere near me when you're in town."

"With good reason, ma," she told her as politely as she could.

"Um huh... well if that's how you feel, your presence isn't missed. I'll see you around, if not, that's fine too." With one last look of disgust, she walked away and out of the building.

Joc watched her disappear, and though she was very thankful, she was hurt too. Ever since she'd been a child her mother had spoken down to her. Nothing Joc ever did was good enough, and her mother made sure to tell her that every chance she got.

Her time spent in juvie was the best thing that could have ever happened to her because it got her moved to Brooklyn, where her father did his best to dote on her and make her feel special. He'd been there for her the best he could emotionally, but her mother had already done so much damage, there wasn't much he could really do to make Joc feel good about herself.

"Don't let her bother you." Uzoma led her back to the table the hostess had set aside for them.

"I'm not. She's always like that. That's nothing new."

"You're beautiful, Jocelynn."

Joc smiled across the table at him. "I know." She touched his hand. "Thanks to you."

"Anybody that doesn't enjoy your existence has a problem

with themselves. I get happy just by looking at you. I don't know how they could live whole lives without you in them. That shit would drive me insane. I couldn't do the shit just being honest." Uzoma told her as he sat back in the chair watching her.

His entire demeanor was amusing to Joc. To listen to him talking about how he couldn't live without her in such a nonchalant way was the cutest thing to her. He spoke about him needing her just as easy as he took his next breath.

"You talk about needing me like it's the most natural thing in the world." Joc stared at him in awe.

He shrugged his shoulders before sitting up and leaning across the table. "That's because it is. Shit, in my world, needing you is like needing oxygen."

"Aww, Uzomaaaaa, you're so sweet," Joc gushed

"Don't even start. You should already know that by now."

Joc propped her face up in the palm of her hand and watched

him lovingly. "I do, but I still like to hear it."

"Well, I'll make sure to keep telling you." He blew her a kiss. "Now pick something to eat, and don't pull that steak and pasta shit like you did at Cheddar's.

Joc laughed for a few minutes before doing as she was told. They spent the afternoon eating and talking before going back to Lu and Brasi's spot. Joc and Lu ended up staying in the house all night, due to the fact that Zino's bachelor party was in full effect. They had no problem with it though, because it had been a minute since they'd hung out.

By the time Uzoma got back, all he wanted to do was lay up under her and have sex. She gave him what he needed before they showered and got back into bed. He was sleep within seconds, thanks to the alcohol in his system. She stayed up a little while longer to make sure all of their things for the wedding was together.

"Baby, get in the bed," Uzoma called out to her sleepily.

"I need to find your socks." She was rummaging through his bag looking for his black dress socks.

"They're in the side pocket, now get in the bed."

Joc checked the side pocket and found them. That satisfied her enough to get her into bed. As soon as she sat on the mattress, Uzoma pulled her to him and fell back to sleep, with her behind him.

***

"Zino, do you take Lonnie as your lawfully wedded wife?" The pastor's voice resonated through the church.

Joc sat in the audience with a bright smile on her face as she watched Zino marry the woman that he described as the woman of his dreams. He looked so happy, almost like a different person. He had been smiling from the moment she'd walked into the room. The look of admiration on his face was indescribable as she walked down the aisle.

Joc didn't even know Lonnie like that, but she couldn't help but to cry when she came in. She was such a beautiful bride, and the love that radiated from her for Zino just made her heart smile. The two of them were so in love that you could feel it just by looking at them. Jocelynn had been on a semi high since she'd gotten there.

"I do." The voices of the men in the church could be heard as they hooped and roared in the typical manly fashion.

Laughter temporarily took over the sanctuary until everyone calmed down enough for the preacher to continue. This time, when Joc looked back to the front of the church, Uzoma was looking at her. He was eyeing her in the way that only he could. It was as if he was talking to her through his eyes. She'd become quite accustomed to it, loved it to death. Their own secret lover's language.

He, Zino, and Lonnie's brother had all gone to the beauty salon that morning to get their hair twisted back into one big French braid for the wedding, and though Zino and Lonnie's brother looked handsome, they had nothing on her baby.

Uzoma was the kind of fine that you couldn't ignore. The way his skin matched his eyes and hair, put together with his height and build, matched with that sexy ass stance and fearless aura he exuded, people had no other choice but to take notice.

The raw and unique beauty that he possessed in that manly way of his commanded the attention of everybody in the room. How and why Zino had chosen him to stand next to him was beyond Joc. If she was Zino, there was no way in the hell she would have put a 6 foot 7 African as uniquely striking as Uzoma next to her on her wedding day.

There was just no competition there, well at least not in Joc's eyes. She might have been the only one with thoughts that absurd running through her mind. Uzoma was the sexiest man on the face of the earth to her, so her opinion was pretty biased anyway.

"You're so fucking sexy," she mouthed to Uzoma as he stood at the front of the church.

The smile on his face let her know that she still had the same effect on him as he had on her. She could even see his cheeks turning a little red from where she was sitting. The magnetic pulling in her chest took off into overdrive as she sat lost in the eyes of her lover, her protector, her saving grace, the love that she felt down in her soul.

Uzoma Youngblood. Her man. He was the epitome of courage, longevity, passion, and love. She'd spent her entire life finding one bad person after the other, only to stumble directly into the path of her soulmate. Though they weren't married yet, she felt it on the inside. Their hearts connected on a level that not even she could explain.

"I now present to you, Mr. and Mrs. Zino Green."

That one statement sent the church into an outburst of cheers and praises. Jocelynn and Uzoma included. Everyone was clearly just as happy for Zino and Lonnie as she was. Smiles and tears were all around the room as Zino grabbed Lonnie's face and kissed her again quickly before grabbing her hand and jumping over the broom that had just been placed in front of them.

Since the wedding was over, people began to file out after the wedding party headed to the reception. Jocelynn followed Lu and Brasi to their table and took her seat, waiting for the partying to resume. She was too big to indulge in any of the festivities for real, but she planned to enjoy herself as soon as Uzoma got in there.

He had already made her promise to dance the night away with him, and she had plans to do just that. She was seated facing the door so that she could Uzoma when he came in. The wedding party had already begun to file in as their names were announced.

All of the groomsmen and bridesmaids had been called, so the last two people to come in before Zino and Lonnie was her sister, then Uzoma. Joc's heart sped up after Lonnie's sister walked in as if she hadn't just seen him a few minutes ago.

She was smiling before they even called his name. All she could see was his shadow against the door, but that was enough for her.

"Lastly, we have the future husband of a Ms. Jocelynn Waters," The DJ announced over the mic.

Joc looked from the door to the DJ then back to the door, but the lights were dimming. In her throat, stuck, was the last breath she had been prepared to take, but it wouldn't come out. Her hands were shaking too badly, and her mind was racing as the last thing she'd expected to happen began to happen.

"Stop looking crazy, Jocelynn, and come here, baby," Uzoma's voice came over the intercom, but she still didn't see him.

"Where are you?" She jumped up and screamed through the room, drawing a few laughs from the attendees.

"Where I've always been. The only place I'll forever be."

Joc stood confused, looking all around the room trying to find him. It was clear that he was no longer at the door because the hostesses had already closed them.

"Uzoma?" She called out to him again, totally disregarding the crowd watching her.

All she cared about was him. She needed him, and that was it.

308

"Just think about it, Jocelynn, where have I been since the moment I saw you?"

Joc's mind was everywhere as she tried to think of where he could be. There was one place she could think of, but that couldn't be it because she didn't see him... or did she? The more she thought about it, the wider her smile became. She spun around to her side and there he stood, in his vest and tuxedo pants with the most infectious smile she'd ever seen.

He was holding the mic in one hand and a ring in the other. It was down by his side but she wouldn't have been able to miss those diamonds even if she'd tried.

"Where am I, baby?"

Joc's tears clouded her eyes and throat as she tried to speak. "By my side," she whispered breathlessly.

"I love you."

She covered her chest and was once again trying to catch her breath as he kneeled on the floor in front of her.

"I love you too, Uzoma,"

"You can't hoe around forever, right baby?"

Joc along with almost everybody in the room laughed. Tears slid down her face as she nodded her head.

"Right."

"A man has to be ready to change for the right woman, huh?"

Joc nodded as she recollected their conversation from the day before.

"Well, baby, I'm ready to change."

Sniffles could be heard around the room as Joc stood there crying uncontrollably.

"Let's love each other forever, Jocelynn." Uzoma grabbed her hand. "Will you marry me?"

"Yessssss." She reached for him, and he stood from the floor before sliding the ring on her finger.

Music began to play as he held her in his arms. People all around them were smiling and clapping as she enjoyed the best moment of her life. Joc cried and kissed all over Uzoma until she felt someone tapping her arm. When she turned around, Lonnie was standing there with her bouquet of flowers.

"Looks like this belongs to you. Congratulations, girl!" She squealed before grabbing Joc for a hug.

Zino followed Lonnie, giving Joc a hug before dapping Uzoma up.

"Nigga, if you're done stealing my day, I'd like to get my reception started now," Zino joked as they held each other in a manly embrace.

Once all the cheers and congratulatory support was given, the reception kicked off, and Joc had the best time of her life.

Epilogue

"Uzoma, make them sit down!" Joc yelled from the porch of her house.

Dakeyo and Deumi were standing on the top of their swing set and scaring the living daylights out of their mother. Uzoma, on the other hand, was standing right next to them and obviously didn't see anything wrong with it.

"Baby, they're boys, leave 'em alone."

"I don't care, Uzoma, they're only two. They are going to hurt themselves."

Lonnie walked past her with a bowl of potato salad. "Girl, stop worrying yourself about them babies, he ain't gon' let nothing happen to them, and you know that."

Though Joc was worried, Lonnie was right. Uzoma was just as protective of their boys as he was of her, and that was saying a lot. He barely let her out of his sight, and it was even worse with them.

"I don't know why she's tripping anyway. Them lil niggas are the size of four year olds," Taryn said as she set the pan of ribs on the table.

"Y'all, I know, but I can't help it." Joc gave them a fake pout as she walked all the way out into the yard.

"I used to be the same way with Ayo, but he'll kill me with all the shit he be doing, so I just let him be now." Taryn sat in her seat at the table.

It was the twins' second birthday, and Joc and Uzoma were having a birthday party for them at the house with just family and friends. Jacko and Kia, Zino and Lonnie, Demoto and Taryn, and even Brasi, Lu, Breon, and Wren had come down to celebrate.

"I hope I don't be that bad." Lonnie rubbed her bulging belly.

"Well, think again." Breon told her. "I'm hopeless,"

"And all of these niggas are the same," Kia chimed in. "They're just being boys, and blah, blah, blah."

The women at the table laughed and joked with each other as the men stood out in the yard tending to their kids. Between everyone there minus Lu and Brasi, who hadn't any luck in the child bearing department, there was a yard full of children.

They were all running around laughing and playing, not paying their overly concerned fathers any attention. Joc had bent over backward planning the boys' party, and was happy to see that it was a success. Five months pregnant with their daughter, the planning had been tiring, but she'd pulled it off.

"What you over here smiling for?" Uzoma walked in front of her and kissed her nose.

"How happy I am."

He grabbed her hand before kissing her forehead. "I told you all you had to do was give me all you had, and I was gon' make you happy."

"I know, but I didn't know you would actually do it."

Uzoma stared at her for a minute before kissing her mouth. "I did it, and I'ma keep on doing it." He kissed her once more before walking away, with her eyes following his every step.

To love and be loved... it wasn't all bad. In fact, it was the best thing that Joc could have ever done. If she had the opportunity, she'd do it all over again, as long as her outcome was Uzoma and the life they'd built together. That was one thing she wanted forever.

The End

CPSIA information can be obtained
at www.ICGtesting.com
Printed in the USA
LVHW04s0958230718
584633LV00001B/128/P